## TRAIL NORTH

Five years after walking out on the family ranch to join a trail herd heading north, young Cal McCale hears his brothers are in trouble. Returning to Texas, he finds family loyalty means nothing; his brothers—the so-called 'Three Tough T's'—have gambled away his share of the ranch and plan to drive the herd over the border to Kansas for a quick sale. Cal must decide who comes first: himself or his brothers. Yet, as the journey begins, there are other enemies waiting to attack, who want to make certain that none of the McCales gets to Kansas alive...

# TRAIL NORTH

## Al Cody, 1899-

Archie Joscelyn, 1899-

**WESTERNS**
RODMAN PUBLIC LIBRARY

First published 1968
by Manor Books Inc.

This hardback edition 1992
by Chivers Press
by arrangement with
Donald MacCampbell Inc.

ISBN 0 7451 4533 7

Copyright, ©, 1967, by Archie Joscelyn
All rights reserved

**British Library Cataloguing in Publication Data available**

Printed and bound in Great Britain by
Redwood Press Limited, Melksham, Wiltshire

# TRAIL NORTH

**Chapter 1**

McCale came upon the wagon trace in the middle of nowhere. These southern fringes of The Nations were wide, as deceptively empty as a discarded plate at a picnic. The grass leaned under the endless push of the wind, disturbed by the mark of wheels. In such country they were almost frightening, like something strayed or lost. Only Indians or renegade whites rode here—or strays like himself, who knew better, or ought to.

This was the wilderness primeval—plain and prairie, lonely with its unending vastness; any man who crossed it took his life in his hands. In McCale's case the risk was minimized, since he rode mostly by night. A wagon was noisy and visible for long distances; in the broad light of day, the still-bending stalks of grass testified that it had passed within the hour.

*Likely it's because there's a town not too far off—or what passes for one,* he reflected. *In any case, I'm not the only fool on the loose.*

Was he foolish, reading too much into a letter of a single paragraph, and setting out for Texas on the strength of it? It had been a statement, not an appeal for help, and not from his brothers. The closer he came to Texas, the deeper grew McCale's conviction that he'd discover anew that he wasn't wanted.

*The Return of the Prodigal*, he thought bitterly —though there had been no riotous living in his three years away from the big spread on the Colorado, and almost certainly there would be no fatted calf killed at his reappearance.

*More likely they'd prefer to kill the prodigal*, he reflected, and this time there was humor about his mouth, the smile of a big man who had found the saving grace of being able to laugh at himself. Perhaps he was foolish to return, but old lures drew as powerfully as magnets. In any case, the letter had arrived when he had business of his own in Texas, so, in a sense, time stood like the sun in the high noonday sky.

Now that sun was slipping into the West, almost ready to run for cover. He topped a long, easy slope, and ahead a lengthening shadow stood alien to the plain. It was the wagon; he swung his horse and touched it to a run, urged as much by curiosity as surprise.

A woman came running toward him, waving a faded shawl above her head to attract his attention, then turning back almost as hurriedly when she saw that he was responding. The wagon, its canvas roof weathered, looked lost and out of place. A man sat in the small patch of shade which it cast, his back to a wheel; his eyes turned slowly under the brim of his hat, following the woman, but beyond that he did not stir. A single bay horse, still harnessed, was tied to a rear wheel.

There had been sign of trouble in the tracks of the wagon, as though the horses ran wildly, out of control. Now trouble was self-evident, and here was folly to match or cap McCale's own—a lone wagon, with two people, on this endless and always hostile plain.

"You folks having trouble, ma'am?" McCale doffed

his hat as he swung to the ground. The woman eyed him intently, the politely conventional gesture not lost on her. Her eyes were very blue and searching, and he submitted to that breathless scrutiny with good grace, still holding his hat in his hand.

Apparently she was satisfied with what she saw: eyes a couple of shades darker than her own, a face which had known the razor no longer ago than the morning, framed by bright hair beginning to need cutting. The big nose was matched by a solid jaw which lacked the traditional stubbornness of the McCales, doubly lightened by the humor at the back of his eyes. For size he was not merely impressive, but almost overwhelming. There was six feet three of him, and the holstered gun at his waist took on the look of a toy.

Words spilled from the woman in a sudden torrent: "Thank God for you, young man! And surely you come as an answer to prayer. For the last half hour I've been praying as I never prayed before, petitioning the Throne of Grace that a miracle might happen—and behold, you come riding! We're in desperate trouble!"

"I'll be glad to help," McCale assured her. "You're hurt?" he asked the man.

"Nought to matter, now that I've got my breath back." The man moved for the first time, aiding himself with hands on the wheel, the big-knuckled hands of a toiler. He pulled himself to a standing position, grimacing and favoring his left leg. "A jackrabbit spooked the horses—jumping from behind a clump of grass like the Devil a-laughin'. They were running crazy before I could hold them. A wheel hit a rock and bounced us crazy, and I was thrown off. I must have hit on my head—my weakest place," he added with a rueful grin. "I was knocked out—and they thought I was killed, or just about."

McCale took note of the plural, but he could see only

the woman, and the one horse; the second horse of the team was missing.

"Ma here, and Carrie—our girl—were plumb upset," the man went on. "Specially when they couldn't revive me for a while. Carrie remembered that we'd passed a town only a few miles off east, and she jumped on one of the horses and took off, hoping to find a doctor. She hasn't come back," he added soberly, "and we're scared. A town like that—any town—is no place for a girl."

McCale nodded agreement. Towns of any sort were few and far between in this country, though Plentywood at least met the requirement as a settlement. More could scarcely be said. Its name was a misnomer, trees being a rarity hereabouts; as for what a town ought to be, it was no better—a stench on the clean prairie wind.

"She's been gone more than an hour," the mother explained urgently. "I should have stopped her, but I guess I wasn't thinking quite straight right then. But of course such a town is no place for a girl to venture alone, even for Carrie. And it's unlikely there will be any doctor."

That was so unlikely that it would border on a miracle; in this land, men lived or died without benefit either of clergy or medicos. In most cases, death was sudden and swift, though whether that could be counted as a blessing was open to question.

"I don't need any doctor, anyhow," the man explained. "I'm still kind of shaky, but I'll be fine. I ain't quite up to settin' that other cayuse yet . . ." He essayed a step and was forced to clutch again at the wheel to steady himself. "Carrie took the only one that's ever been ridden. If it ain't askin' too much, and you could see your way clear to going after her . . ."

"We'll be everlastingly grateful to you, sir," Carrie's

mother confirmed. She added poignantly, "I'm afraid for her."

McCale nodded; there was reason for apprehension. He swung back to the saddle. "I'll find her," he promised. "Carrie—what's her last name?"

"Dulane, Carrie Dulane. You'll know her by her hair—yellow as the sun, off there, or your own." The sun was like a ball, bouncing at the rim of the prairie. "It may be a risky chore, boy!"

McCale smiled. "Rest easy," he said. "I've a bone, from far back, to pick with that town."

*Not much of a bone, actually,* he reflected, urging his horse to a run. That had happened five years ago, when he was sixteen, already man-sized and long accustomed to doing a man's work. He'd been offered a chance to go along north with a trail herd, and his brothers had refused him permission; so he'd gone, anyway.

The herd had camped for a night a mile from Plentywood, and that evening, most of the crew had ridden into town. Trouble had erupted when the citizenry had tried to charge double the going prices for everything. McCale hadn't been particularly interested in booze or its cost, but he'd stood with his fellow-Texans long enough to discover that the town's reputation was deserved. Any way you took it, Plentywood was tough.

It belonged to a man named Harms, the town and everything in it—including the people. Harms had surprised the Texas crew by getting the drop on them, laughing, taunting. McCale had turned the tables, managing partly because he was a kid and not watched or taken too seriously. He'd picked up Harms and held him helpless—and Harms had sworn that someday, when McCale was old enough, he'd kill him.

McCale wondered now if Harms was still there, if

Plentywood was still his town. Half a decade was a long while, but Harms would not have forgotten.

Carrie. It was the first time he'd ever heard the name, and it touched a chord, like plucking a fiddle by chance and making music. Carrie, with hair like the sun! An impulsive young girl, riding to get help for her father, not thinking of herself. Not showing very good judgment, perhaps, but under the circumstances, not to be blamed. Only foolish—and doubly so, to ride into Plentywood at the hour of sunset.

Remembering Harms, McCale scratched with the spurs. Counting the time of his own arrival at the wagon, it added up to a time differential of at least a couple of hours. He looked to where the sun had been, and regretted the long siesta he'd indulged in that day. But maybe Carrie's mother was still praying then—and she said her prayer had been answered.

The oncoming night and McCale reached town at the same time. The spreading tide of drabness smoothed out under the darkness, as it cloaked the meanness festering behind unpainted walls. Even so, the town remained as ugly as a toadstool growth; tar paper, curled and warped on the roofs and sides of cabins, showed streaked and torn where sun and wind had worried.

McCale halted at the livery barn near the edge of town, tied his cayuse to the chewed hitch-rail, then stepped inside and bought a feed bag full of oats. That gave him opportunity to question the stableman.

"I'm looking for a girl—my sister," he added with sudden inspiration. "She rode in a while ago, looking for a doctor. Girl with yellow hair. I was off hunting when the accident happened to Pa," he went on. "She should have been back."

The stableman scrubbed at his stubbled chin with the

heel of a flinty palm. A flicker which seemed cousin to sympathy showed in his eyes.

"Your sister?" he repeated; that put a different face on the matter. "Why—yes, as a matter of fact, a girl did come in a while ago. Guess she's somewhere around yet." He jerked a thumb toward a stall. "There's the horse she rode."

"Yeah," McCale agreed. The pony matched the other in the team. They were wiry cayuses, rather small for a work team, but probably they managed to snake the wagon tirelessly across flat or merely rolling country. "You know where she is?" he asked directly.

The stableman's jaws ceased a slow, rotary motion, working up and down for an instant. He sized McCale anew, observing his size and the used look of gun and holster. If he was impressed, it was only with the odds. Sympathy was now plain in his voice and face. He swung an arm.

"Off there, I reckon," he said. "That row of shacks."

McCale nodded. "I'll take her horse along. Have it handy."

The stableman chewed violently, paused, and then threw on a saddle in silence. He led the horse out, passing over the reins. His voice was heavy.

"It was a mistake, her coming to this town," he observed. "We ain't got no medico. Never did have one. And Harms—this town belongs to him. Only he ain't a man; he's a devil. You watch out, boy, he'll kill you."

"Thanks for telling me." McCale hadn't been frightened five years ago, but he *was* scared now; so much hinged on this, far beyond himself. He walked, leading the horses. He was thankful for the darkness, and he walked as though he would shove it back.

He chose the middle of the street in preference to the

plank walk, his boots soundless in the night. Lights shone in the single saloon, where the trail crew had visited that other time. There was no outward change in the town; even the stench which hovered above it still clung, an affront to the nostrils.

Selecting another hitch-rail, he tied the horses, not quite certain how to proceed. But he had a fleeting thought that for once his brothers might approve of what he was doing. Probably they'd call him a fool, as usual, but they should like it.

From inside a dimly lit house he heard a voice, and halted; when it came again he was sure. Carrie's voice matched her mother's, anxious, quick, and passionate —the same inflections, the same quality of muted strength. Somehow it reminded him of a bird at dawn.

"Thanks for the supper—you've been very kind—but now I must be going. I've stayed too long already . . ."

A laugh answered, soft, lazily amused, holding no humor at all. Harms had laughed that way as he eyed the Texans along the barrels of leveled guns.

"Do you think I'd let you go, girl? Now that you've come here? I watched you come riding in, and I couldn't believe my eyes. Such luck don't come often in this country, but when it does, I don't let it slip through my fingers. Besides, it's too dark to ride anywhere . . ."

The voice broke off as McCale knocked, his knuckles rolling like a drum against the brittle wood. There had been a sudden flurry, a sound of struggle, as when cat or owl pounces.

That stopped also, and for a tortured moment the night seemed to hold its breath. Then he heard a gasp, the sound of tearing cloth, and the door was flung open. Carrie stood, framed in the half-light from a smoking coal-oil lamp on a stand at one side. She was tall for a woman, her slenderness enhanced by the flash of white flesh along her upper arm where the sleeve had ripped away. Her hair caught the light and made a halo for her face; this was her mother in a younger edition, eyes wide between terror and desperate hope.

Harms was shadowy in the background, powerful with the controlled grace of a puma, fury held in leash.

"I've come for you, Carrie," McCale said. "Pa and Ma sent me. They're worried about you."

She hadn't known what to expect, and it took a moment for her to adjust. She leaned forward, peering; the light slipped past her shoulder and caught the taut planes of the man's face, revealing the big nose and strong jaw. She studied him desperately, hopefully, and her verdict was like her mother's. Her voice was like the cry of a whippoorwill, wheeling in the darkening sky.

"You—you came for me?"

"Of course. To take you back to the wagon. Your pa's going to be all right."

A second time her breath caught, sharply, painfully. He could see the movement at her throat as she swallowed, while one hand fluttered toward her mouth like an injured bird. "I—of course. I'm ready . . ."

Harms's voice broke in, pushing at them from the gloom of the room behind—a high, tight voice, half-mocking, half-angry. Once heard, it wasn't easily forgotten.

"Where do you think you're going, girl? Do you think I'd let you go—ride out with a man you don't know? You told me there were only your folks and yourself. I'm not that big a fool, even if you are. Besides, I never let anyone go."

"You're letting *her* go," McCale informed him softly. "And you're forgetting something, Harms—some who rode out whether you liked it or not, a few years ago!"

Harms's breath caught jerkily, and he leaned forward,

his face going pale. Recognition flared in his eyes.

"Why you—so you've come back . . ."

"Right," McCale agreed tersely. "You always knew I would, didn't you?"

He saw the light flame higher against the darkness of Harms's eyes, the temptation and struggle, and the shadow of a doubt. Harms's laugh came again.

"I really ought to kill you," he said, "but maybe you're still a trifle young for dying—and riding as a knight-errant! So this once I'll overlook your folly. Get going, Mister—and don't drag your feet!"

## Chapter II

Harms was beside Carrie in the doorway. His hand dropped to her shoulder, twisting her savagely back into the room. McCale heard her gasp, partly in pain, half in fear; he flung himself forward, and as he went the light was puffed out, leaving a blackness in which he sensed rather than saw the swipe of a clubbed gun.

He twisted to the side and came up under the blow, hands reaching out. There was a gun in his own holster, but he felt no need for it. He felt the glancing edge of the other weapon, caught and twisted, a numbing pain running through hand and arm at the impact. It came loose and he struck back with it, still unable to see in the press of close quarters. The second shock of striking was almost as savage as the first.

Now he could see, in the light from the doorway. Harms stood an instant, his face a sudden mask of red, then he sagged to his knees and prostrated himself across the doorway. A thin, high shriek reached through the town; at that summons, the street, deserted one moment, sprang alive and venomous, before the sound could die.

"Come, girl," McCale commanded, and at the urgency in his voice she was beside him, leaping the barrier of the fallen man, outside and running. Muted whisperings from a blacker huddle erupted into an ugly roar; a gun flung crimson challenge.

McCale's hand was recovering from its numbness. He turned, lifting the weapon he'd torn from Harms, reaching for his own with his other hand. Three guns were hammering lead toward them, three men working the triggers. Those were Harms's bodyguard, stumbling from the saloon at the summons, the trio who had terrorized the town.

McCale's guns were slower, deliberate and deadly. Then he sensed Carrie beside him, her voice shaking as she begged him to come. He caught her up and boosted her onto her own horse, jerked the reins loose, flinging the empty gun where a shadow moved, and reached his own horse. The cayuses sprang to a run.

Turmoil seethed and frothed behind them, loudness making a substitute for courage. As they reached the outskirts, McCale reached and grasped the reins of Carrie's horse, turning both animals. They thundered back the way they had come, scattering men and horses along the street. This time, the confusion was so complete that no shots were fired.

Carrie gasped as the horses settled to running. "But we're going the wrong way!"

"Sure," McCale agreed. "We'll swing as soon as we lose them."

She voiced no further protest as he slowed the horses and turned again. They waited in the shadows of an old barn as a pursuit was finally organized and other horsemen pounded past. After the sounds had died, they moved quietly out.

Carrie stifled her impulse to hurry, realizing that haste might draw attention. She cast curious looks at this calm man who had outmatched a town, but she asked no questions. Voices could carry a long way.

He held the horses to a walk until far beyond the town, then put them to a run. Clouds had blotted out the moon. "Luck's with us, tonight," he observed.

"You mean I'm lucky—that you came along." Carrie drew a long, sighing breath. "I don't even know who you are—to—to thank you. And you—you must think I'm—terribly foolish."

"Why, no," he denied. "I was just thinking how much spunk you have to go after help the way you did. I had a talk with your folks 'fore I came on to try and find you."

"And Pa—you said he was better?"

"He was up and talking again. And they were worried about you."

She drew a long breath. "I guess I acted without stopping to think. But he—he looked awful bad. And we'd seen the town off there . . ."

"You did the natural thing. Only trouble is that such towns are good places to stay clear of." To ease her embarrassment, he shifted the subject. "I'm glad I happened along as I did. I'm Cal McCale—headin' home, you might say, for Texas."

"McMcCale? Texas?" A thread of excitement wove through her voice. "Why, we stopped at a ranch in Texas—the Muleshoe. A big outfit on the Colorado, run by three brothers, and their name is McCale."

He turned to look more closely at her, wishing that the light was better.

"They wouldn't be three long-whiskered patriarchs, like Abraham, Isaac, and Jacob? With black beards reaching clear to their waists?"

"Yes, that's them," she agreed excitedly. "Are they really your brothers? How odd to meet you here! You've just helped me—and they helped us, too, with supplies, some of which were hard to get. Like powder and shot, for Pa's old muzzle-loader. There were a lot of things we needed, and your brother Tom said we might as well take them, that the stuff had just been kicking around, cluttering up. I guess he could tell that we were pretty hard up."

McCale felt warmed. Stuff had a way of collecting, of course, until it became junk; but however small a thing such a gift might be, still it was something for which he could be proud of his brothers. And there had not been too many things in the past.

"You mean you folks have come all the way up from Texas? And you're travelin' alone?"

"Yes. Ma and I were with relatives in the Ozarks for a while, while Pa looked around. When he got a house fixed up at a place to suit him, he came to fetch us. We're going there now. And Pa, he more or less prefers to travel alone."

He caught the unconscious note of pathos and resignation, but made no comment. It was none of his business, of course, though even a self-centered, fiddle-footed man should give more thought to his family and less to his own inclinations. It was one thing for a man like McCale himself to travel alone, but quite another to go out with a single wagon and a couple of women.

Still, it was free country. and folks could do as they pleased. At least, until someone interfered—someone like Harms.

An eye winked like a star, low against the horizon. Guided by the beacon of the campfire, they reached the wagon. Mrs. Dulane was touchingly grateful. Dulane gripped McCale's hand, muttering wordlessly. The news that he was a brother to the McCales of Texas made it seem as though they were old friends.

McCale accepted their invitation to roll in his blanket near the wagon, and he slept lightly, as was his custom.

By daylight, with excitement coloring her cheeks, Carrie was as pretty as he'd been certain she would prove.

There was a wistful note in her voice as she said good-bye and the wagon went on, and he swallowed a lump in his throat as he watched them out of sight. For the second time in weeks of riding, he was uncertain in mind.

He loitered until the following morning, making sure that there was no pursuit from Plentywood. Apparently they'd had their fill already. Still half-regretful, he resumed his own journey, south by west. The only trouble was that all the hope and luster had gone out of the ride.

It was a far piece from Montana to Texas, a ride McCale had more than half made up his mind never to take again. Or, if he did, he'd figured that it would be to another part of Texas, far shy of the Colorado and the Muleshoe. Texas offered room enough without crowding or letting the other McCales know of his journeyings. But Texas cattle would be fine for stocking his own spread, a long curve of land along the Yellowstone, north by west from Fort Keogh.

But the letter, postmarked from Catclaw, had changed his mind about going back. It was even reason enough to continue south when a strong impulse stirred in him to ride along, instead, with the Dulanes, to more or less make sure that they arrived at their destination in good shape.

As for the letter, he had no idea who had written it. It had been unsigned, but blunt and to the point:

> *Your brothers are in trouble—and it's likely to turn out to be more than they can chew. Being a McCale yourself, maybe you won't care. And of course they'd choke on it before they'd ever admit to such a thing.*

That somewhat twisted phrase described them so well that he couldn't doubt the probable truth of the letter. Having been minded to ride for Texas anyhow, he'd set out without delay. Maybe—just maybe—they'd be glad to see him this time. It was unlikely, but it was a chance.

Texas stretched interminably, perhaps because he kept thinking about a lone wagon heading on across the empty plains. The trouble was that the plains were not empty, but might erupt in violence at any time. In retrospect, McCale knew that he should have asked more questions, pinpointing their destination, offering at least a little advice. He was pretty sure that it would not have been out of place.

Dulane wanted a piece of land, where, as he put it, a man could have room to breathe in. Apparently he'd spent years in the search; he even thought he'd found it. It was another manifestation of mountain fever, the incurable sort.

The belated realization of his own shortcomings turned McCale blue. He'd passed up his chance; and the probability of ever finding that lone cabin, or Carrie, was so remote as to be hardly a possibility.

The town of Catclaw lay at the edge of the Muleshoe spread, which was by way of saying that it was a good distance from the ranch buildings. It baked in the early summer sun as he rode up.

Mart Reul, who ran the store, eyed him with mild surprise.

"I was wondering would you maybe be riding in one of these days," he volunteered. "So those stubborn brothers of yours finally bowed their stiff necks enough to send for you, eh?"

"I haven't been asked by them to come back," McCale confessed. "Is something wrong?"

"Wrong, is a mild word," Reul snorted. "I reckon you know their besetting sin—among other failings. And for stubbornness, they'd make a balky mule seem right down eager. Maybe you can talk some sense into their heads —though I doubt it."

McCale held the same doubts. The matter seemed

reasonably clear, since their besetting sin was a love of gambling. Like some types of drunkards who could lay off for a time, Tom, Tim, and True McCale could go for long periods without a turn of the cards. But every so often they would break loose in a binge, a game which might last out the day and far into the night. Some of those games had become legendary.

The three played as a team, and sometimes they won, sometimes they lost. Across the years, they had become increasingly poor losers, and insufferable winners. Either way, their reputation in the community was not enhanced.

It was midafternoon when he sighted the ranch buildings. Squat and old, they gave the impression of tired horses dozing in the sun. He'd hoped to get a lift out of these last miles, a sense of homecoming, but all that he felt was a matching feeling of emptiness. No one was waiting to greet him. Since they hadn't sent for him, that was not to be expected, but it was strange that he could ride across the empty land unnoticed.

A thin lift of smoke came from the cook house, and a half-dozen saddled horses rested their heads above the hitching rail. He read the brands automatically as he dismounted, and none were Muleshoe.

A murmur of voices drifted from the big abode. A screen door was thick with flies, the inner door standing open. He let himself in, dodging quickly to keep out the disturbed flies, then pushed on to the dimness of wide, low rooms, of thick walls and a comfortable coolness, even on hot days.

The voices came from the next room. One he recognized without difficulty. It belonged to Tom, the oldest of The Three Tough T's, as his brothers took pride in being known. All three had been grown when he was born, and Tom was the oldest, had always been the boss. Quick and arrogant in making decisions, he was harshly stubborn in sticking to them. Today his voice held an odd quality.

"You figure to give us no choice, of course. But if you hadn't come here like a pack of cowards—thieves in the night . . ."

"Now, now, Tom, take it easy!" The answering voice was measured, reasonable. "We didn't sneak in on you. We rode openly, and who has a better right? You boys gambled again last night—remember?—and this time, we won! And you aren't suggesting that the game was crooked, or any part of it—now are you?"

True answered—Truman McCale, the youngest of The Three T's. His voice was choked with the same sense of outrage. "You won, so let it go at that!"

"Why, sure, True, sure—that's what we figured to do, to let it go at that. Unless, of course, you fellows want to put another stake on the board—the big one, maybe? Last night, you didn't seem to want to, but maybe you've thought it over and changed your minds? We're willing to be reasonable, to meet you halfway, any time."

"The hell with you," Tim exploded. "You had the luck, so let it go at that. We've learned one thing, and that's when to quit! You ought to be satisfied with your luck."

"Why, yes, I guess we are, if that's the way you feel. But we *did* win last night. And so, instead of you boys being proprietors of the Bent Elbow, like you hoped, why, we own the Muleshoe now. If you'd won, you'd have taken over the saloon, right then and there. Since we won, we've come to take over. But without pushing you boys, of course, and no hard feelings."

McCale was beginning to get the picture. His brothers had staked the ranch against the saloon, and the cards had gone against them. Now, Tim talked virtuously of knowing when to quit!

McCale could see the roomful of men. As usual, his

brothers easily dominated the gathering—tall, powerful men, heavy black beards sweeping to their waists, wide black hats set low on their heads. True stood three inches above Tom and Tim, though he was still that much shorter than the McCale who was not a T. All three emanated power. There was a sprinkling of gray along the temples of the three, a hint of frost in the beard of Tom. Otherwise, the years had worked no outward change.

The ranch crew stood with them—Sam Tucker, Slim Bledsoe, Gil Jenkins, and others, new since his day. They were matched in number by the crew who had ridden out from town. The spokesman, whose back was to McCale, wore a black frock coat and looked like a gambler, but he had the air of a gentleman. Watchful hostility marked the two groups.

"What the devil are we going to do with a herd and no range?" Tim blurted suddenly.

The gambler shrugged, a quizzical smile lifting the mustache at the corners of his mouth. "Now that's a good thought," he conceded. "Perhaps you boys should have given some thought to it before you played last night. But if you wish to put another stake on the table—we're willing to accommodate you."

"We're through," Tom announced harshly. "We take our losses, no more. And I've turned my last card for as long as I live."

"Well, if that's the way you feel about it, don't accuse us of poor sportsmanship!" The gambler was restraining himself with difficulty. "And since that's your decision, you'll have to find new range for your herd. Not that we intend to crowd you."

"Thanks for nothing," Tom growled. "All right, we'll start rounding them up in the morning, and move out as fast as we can—though where, I don't know."

"That's fine with us. And now, if you don't mind, we'll

look the place over before we return to town."

"Look all you please; it's yours,"Tom snapped, then stared as he caught sight of the watcher behind them. "Where in blazes did you come from?" he demanded. Then, to the question in the eyes of the others, he made a grudging introduction. "Strang, this is our kid brother —Calvin McCale. There's one thing a man can always depend on. Trouble always comes in bunches!"

## Chapter III

Cal shrugged as he accepted Strang's handshake. He found himself liking the man, yet repelled at the same time; here was a strange mixture.

"Kid brother, did you say?" Strang repeated, and glanced at the trio. "All I can say is, he may be the youngest, but he's certainly no runt, Tom."

"That's a matter of opinion," Tom returned harshly.

The others went out, sweeping aside the clustered flies with the brush of a big hat. There were nods from some of the crew, low-voiced welcomes from Tucker, Bledsoe, and Jenkins, but no further greeting, no welcome or even curiosity from his brothers as to why he had returned. Nothing, he realized bitterly, had changed in the years he'd been away. He was still the Kid, the unwanted one, not one of the Three who did all the thinking and made all the decisions.

It was an old story. Tom had been twenty when he was born; Tim and True had followed Tom at yearly intervals. They had been The Three Tough T's even then, separated from him by much more than the wide variance in ages.

Cal was the baby of the family, and they had always treated him like one. Even when, at fifteen, he had exceeded all of them in growth and strength, the added physical prowess had only enhanced their feelings. They had always resented him, perhaps unconsciously, but blaming him because their mother had died when he was born. They had loved their mother, and had never forgiven him.

For most of their lives, the three had worked together. As a team, they made all decisions, though Tom remained the boss. While a boy, motherless and fatherless, Cal had accepted that as right and proper; it was only when he had reached sixteen, and they had still insisted on treating him as a kid, that he had grown resentful. By then, he'd overtowered them all, and could ride any horse on the ranch, rope, tie, or brand any steer, outride, outwalk, and outwork any other man in that part of Texas. Except in their eyes. Never in their eyes.

Refused permission to travel north with a trail herd being rodded by a neighbor, he'd gone, anyhow; that summer had been a toughening experience. And it had been his work, more than any other man's, which had gotten the herd and the crew through—not alone at Plentywood, but when disaster had overtaken them farther along.

Returning to Texas, he had expected, at long last, to be accepted as one of the McCales. But nothing had been changed; in the eyes of his brothers he was still a green kid. He had tried hard to please them, hoping to show them that he was a man, one of them. Finally, in disgust, he'd pulled out a second time, and only now was he returning.

Now he was a man in the eyes of the law, as well as of others with whom he'd worked, and he knew that he'd made the ride from Montana as much in the hope of setting things right as in response to that letter. It had all the earmarks of a vain wish, but he'd give it the best try he knew.

After Strang and his partners had ridden away, the three discussed their problem, ignoring him. He was about to turn away when True suddenly snarled a question:

"You claim to be a man—so why'd you just stand there after you found out what was going on? They walked in on us and caught us flat-footed—but you could have got the drop on them!"

Cal eyed them in amazement, wondering for a moment if True was serious. It was apparent that he was.

"Why, I suppose I might have," he acknowledged. "I didn't think of making such a play. Was that what you wanted?"

"It's a poor man who won't fight for his own!" Tom snapped.

"When it's a matter for a fight, yes. But the way I heard it, you bet the ranch against the saloon—and lost. Are you meaning that you'd welch on your bet?"

All three faces reddened around the fringes of whisker.

"Keep a civil tongue between your teeth, Kid!" Tom growled.

"Civil, is it? Does the truth hurt that much? What's got into you fellows, anyhow? I ought to knock your heads together and maybe pound some sense into them. Or is that too much to expect? Sure—I could have got the drop on Strang and his crew. And if you want a war, after losing your bet, you can still start one. But I wouldn't fight in it."

"After what we've just seen, we wouldn't expect that," Tim said. "You'd be scared to!"

He'd been resolved to avoid argument when he returned, but such treatment was going too far.

"I like to know what I'm fighting for," he said mildly. "And if there's anything to be gained. A dead horse ain't worth quarreling over, and it strikes me that's what Muleshoe is. I've traveled across a lot of country in the last few years. Now that the war's over, and with so many people having lost everything they had, they're starting to swarm west like a horde of grasshoppers, looking for free land and a chance at a fresh start. And at the rate they're moving, it won't be many years till the free range is gone."

True gave him a peculiar look. "What's that got to do with us?"

"Do you have to ask? Muleshoe is a big outfit, but it's cattle and graze, range which Pa pre-empted and you've held on to. Taking and holding it hasn't been too hard, when nobody else really wanted it. But you've no deed to the land, no legal title. Right now, the homesteaders are heading this way—I've seen some of them the last few days! When they come, trying to stop them from taking over will be a losing argument."

"Phaw!" True scoffed. "No fool nesters could run us out! There's ways of dealing with them!"

"I've seen others who thought the same. When I first went north with a trail herd, we crossed some outfits who talked the same way. But some of that country is settled now and under the plow, a day's ride from east to west! Herds have to swing a hundred miles farther west than what they did. You can stop one man, or maybe a dozen, but you can't stop them when they come by the scores and hundreds. What I'm saying is that this land isn't worth fighting over—expecially after losing it on a bet!"

He caught the same look between them again, a mixture of slyness and triumph. Tim shrugged. "All right, you're talking. You got some notion of what we ought to do, maybe?"

Tim's attitude might be a trap, but it gave him a chance to suggest what he'd had in mind all along. "From what I could gather, you still have the cattle. That so?"

"Do you think we'd be crazy enough to risk the cattle on the turn of a card?" Tom countered.

"No, I didn't think so, and there you showed mighty good sense. So, drive the herd north. There's still plenty of open range in Montana, and it's good cattle country. I've gotten hold of a spread, and there's plenty of grass and water, along with winter shelter. From the talk, it won't be too long till there'll be a railroad, which will solve marketing problems. All that the land lacks is cattle to run on it. If we put the two together, we'll have a better spread than ever . . ."

"Are you crazy?" Tom demanded incredulously. "Drive to Montana—that wasteland of wolves and blizzards? Why, cattle couldn't survive such winters. You can have your spread to run coyotes on. Maybe you can find a market for rattlesnakes! But you'll never see any of *our* stock up there!"

"Your trouble, Tom, is that you've listened to too many tall tales by too many people who've never even set eyes on that country," Cal replied patiently. "But I've been there. I've lived on that land for the last three years—and so has a fair-sized herd of critters. I've spent the winters there as well as the summers, and I tell you . . ."

"You'll tell us nothing, Kid!" Tom snapped. "I say we won't go to Montana, and that's final! We'll drive north all right—as far as the railroad that's building across Kansas. Once we hit that, we'll ship them to Chicago and sell, and be shut of the whole blasted mess!"

Again, those glances of sly triumph flicked between them, and Cal clamped his lips. It was plain that they had already discussed this between themselves and decided on their course of action. Tom's, as always, was the final pronouncement; argument was useless. This time, they had listened to what he had to say, but only enough to get a partial and distorted picture; and they had heard him that far only to get a better chance to slap him down.

He was strongly tempted to turn his back and ride away, never to return. The suspicion that that was what they expected and hoped for made him hesitate. There was something wrong here, something strange—as there had been, now that he thought back with open eyes, through all the years.

They were going to need help whether they could recognize it or not. Equally to the point, he was entitled to his share of the herd, as one of the McCales. If he made a final break now, the herd would be lost, and his heritage with it.

If they really hoped to get rid of him so easily, they were going to be disappointed.

## Chapter IV

It became increasingly plain to Cal McCale during the next few days that in the eyes of The Three Tough T's, nothing was changed. He could stick around if he wanted to—as when he had been a boy—and do his share of the work. But it was still Tom who gave the orders, who made all the decisions, and from them there was no more appeal than from a decree of the Medes and Persians. Even Tim and True dared not question his pronouncements.

The roundup progressed, as they had promised Strang and his companions that it would. Cal noted that one or another of the trio was mysteriously absent much of the time. Of course, there were preparations to be made for a drive, even as far as Kansas, and many matters to be finally wound up. Still . . . he wondered. But he was too proud to ask, and they volunteered no information.

Only once did they warm a little, evincing interest when he mentioned his encounter with the Dulanes.

"They were all three of them mighty grateful to you folks," he added. "They said you'd been good to them, with supplies and all."

Tom cleared his throat self-consciously. "Shucks, all that we did was to put them up for a few days, and let them have some old junk that they figured they could use. They seemed to be nice folks—only lackin' in good sense. I told him there was plenty of good land a lot closer than where he was headin' back for, with neighbors for his womenfolks as well. But that was just what he didn't want—neighbors. Admitted that if there was anybody closer'n a three days' ride in any direction, he felt crowded."

On that point, Cal was in agreement with the three, but it seemed to be the only matter. Then, unexpectedly, Tom sought him out.

"We'll be pulling out with the herd, first thing in the morning," he explained. "Headin' for Kansas and the railroad. Cattle ought to bring a good price, back in Chicago or other points. Getting the herd trail-broke will keep us pretty busy for a while. So if you don't mind, you can go to town and tend to a few last-minute chores. Then you can catch up. That way, it'll save us a day or two."

Since even such small confidence seemed a step in the right direction, Cal agreed. Later, he mentioned the arrangement to Gil Jenkins, who stopped to eye him strangely. "You mean that you're going to town, by yourself—after the rest of us have pulled out?"

"That's the idea," Cal agreed. "But why not? I've ridden quite a lot by myself these last few years."

"*All* your years, far's I've been able to observe," Jenkins agreed. "It's been runnin' in my mind that maybe I made a mistake, sendin' you that letter."

"So it was you, Gil? I sort of guessed as much. But why?"

"I had my reasons. Like I said, I figured they was maybe bitin' off a bigger hunk of trouble than they could chew, and I figured you had some rights in the situation. But maybe it was a mistake to drag you in, after you were shut of the whole mess."

"Why?" Cal repeated patiently.

"Well, like what you just told me, for one thing. Maybe

you've noticed that those three ain't mellowed much since you saw them last?"

"Now you mention it, they aren't what you'd call overripe."

Jenkins snorted. "Those three grow more cantankerous by the day! There was a time when I had hopes of 'em, but time either churns the milk of human kindness to butter or else it curdles!"

Cal hid a smile. "But you are loyal enough to stay with them, no matter what," he pointed out.

"Well, I suppose you could put it that I ain't got no better sense. I've spent most of my life workin' for Muleshoe, and after a while, it gets to be a habit. But that's no excuse for you to get the dirty end of the stick. And, much as I've come to despise them, still, I never thought they'd pull such a dirty trick on you."

"Trick? What do you mean?"

"Make it a whole fistful of tricks—like palmed cards. Back when I wrote you that letter, they'd been gambling again—and that time they'd won. Which didn't add any to their popularity in the community."

"Are you implyin' that their winning wasn't on the up and up?"

"Nope, not that." Jenkins tugged soberly at an ear lobe. "That's a funny thing—they'll pull a crooked trick one way and hee-haw like a jackass, thinkin' it's so funny. But when it comes to gamblin', they do that on the square, figurin' it's a matter of honor. What I'm gettin' at is that they won something which was supposed to be worth a whole lot. Just what it was, I ain't quite sure. There was a whole sack of phony jewels involved in the deal—one of these little buckskin bags that the Indian squaws do a lot of fancy beadwork on. Rubies, diamonds, and stuff—glass beads, I guess. That was a part of it, and they was plenty mad. They sure figured that Strang and his partners had put something over on them. The funny thing is, I have the impression that Strang feels the same way about them!"

"You're kind of losin' me in the tall grass, Gil."

"That makes two of us. I ain't been able to get it straight, with everybody being so close-mouthed, but the one thing I know for sure is that there's more bitter feeling than the venom of a nest of rattlesnakes. And now this—them aimin' to leave you right in the middle, sort of a sacrificial offering!"

"Seems like the more you talk, Gil, the less I know."

Jenkins smiled without humor. "The day you came, you was talkin' about nesters—homesteaders. Well, those three wan't so surprised or unbelievin' as they let on. They're pretty cute—or at least, they think they are!"

"Maybe if you talk long enough . . ."

"Sure, sure, you think I'll come to a point. Which is what I'm doing. What I'm getting at is that they knew they'd lost the spread, and that Strang would be taking over. They figure they got cheated on that previous gamblin' deal, so they've been plotting a way to get even. They knew that nesters were on the way and would soon be right in this part of the country. That's why they're not really opposed to giving up the land to Strang, gambling debt or not."

"In other words, let the rats have a sinking ship."

"Sounds to me like you got that twisted somewhere, but it's the right idea. They're pulling out at midnight with the herd—soon as the moon rises! By morning, they'll be gone, and by the time you reach Catclaw to tend to those few little piddlin' errands, why—*there'll be more'n a hundred nesters swarmin' in and across Muleshoe, squatting on the range, filing on the land*—grabbing the whole outfit, right out from under Strang's nose! And all legal and proper, of course, since—like you told them—it's free range, and open to filing."

McCale listened, appalled. "And they know all this?"

"Cal, they not only know about it, but they've made all the arrangements! True met some of the nesters 'way off east, and fixed up the whole deal. The nesters are at the border now, but keeping out of sight, timin' it to get the jump on Strang! That's the way the Three T's figure to pay him back for cheating them. Maybe it's a smart trick—but the McCales have enjoyed a dwindlin' popularity in this part of Texas for a long while, which ain't a patchin' to how they'll fall in public estimation after this! And I wasn't usin' the words 'sacrificial offerin' ' in jest. You show up in town at that precisely wrong moment, and, being a McCale, you'll be hustled under the nearest tree and given a going-away party. Only you won't go no farther'n you can dance a jig with your head in the air and your feet off the ground!"

"It can't be that bad!" Cal protested. "Maybe they'd like to see me run into trouble, but not to be lynched."

"If you think I'm exaggerating, you go ahead and show up there! I tell you, those three are sour as old swill. Stay behind, if you like—but don't let them see you in town."

After considering all the angles, McCale did as Jenkins advised. The plot was appalling, and that they had included him in such fashion was more bitter than all that had gone before. He'd ridden back to Texas in the hope of a better understanding, and so bitter a reaction on their part was hard to understand.

Keeping his own counsel, he watched the herd pull out at midnight, instead of daylight. Shortly thereafter, he saw the homesteaders appear and spread across the land, setting their stakes, writing out notices. Still later, he observed the reaction as Strang and his bunch discovered, too late, how they had been hoaxed.

Somewhat to his surprise, there was no immediate reaction, no pursuit by those newly double-crossed. But if

Cal was any judge of such men, the vials of their wrath, tightly stoppered, would be like fermenting wine. This was a violent game the McCales played; being a McCale, he was in on it.

It was evening of the next day when he caught up with the herd. Guilt, surprise, and uneasiness were in the faces of the Three T's as he made his appearance, but they asked no questions. Taciturn as well, Cal volunteered nothing. Gil Jenkins gave him a wink and a grin.

The next morning, he was assigned to a place in the dust of the drag. They looked surprised and uncertain when he accepted without complaint.

For several days, they moved with apprehension clinging like a shadow, one which, instead of vanishing at sundown, seemed to push inside their clothes. Then, as the miles lengthened across Texas and nothing happened, Cal saw how their vigilance relaxed, and his own increased. One day he heard the three chuckling over the trick they had pulled as a going-away present.

"They'll remember the McCales in Texas," Tim gritted. "And they thought they could put one over on us!"

"You figure they've given up trying?" Cal asked dryly, and they swung, startled and angry, as he joined the circle. "I doubt they'll give up that easy."

"If they dared try anything, they'd have done it before now," True said confidently. "Before we could get out of reach."

"What's a few miles, or days, or weeks, for that matter?" Cal countered. "And what do they have to stay for, back there, now? You ever think of that?"

"You squawk like an old hen," Tim said uncomfortably.

"Maybe so. It's better to squawk while your head's still attached to your neck. I've noticed riders off on the horizon a couple of times, yesterday and today. Like they were maybe looking over the herd, but taking good care not to be seen themselves.''

"But you saw them?" Tom sneered.

"I was looking for something of the sort."

"If you don't want to risk riding with us, you can always head off by yourself," was the ungracious retort. Cal let it go at that. But whether they realized it or not, the trail north was a long one; and it could well prove to be a cold one as well.

Something was wrong. It was like a bad dream, a nightmare which refused to be shaken off. It had long been a habit with Cal to come wide-awake on the instant, ready to face up to whatever the day might hold. This time, it was different—a heavy struggle, as though he might not awaken at all.

Slowly and painfully, he struggled through enshrouding fog toward consciousness. It was as desperate a fight as he had ever indulged in, a struggle of half-conscious will back toward life. Hammers seemed to beat inside his skull, while saws rasped raggedly across his nerves.

Then he was awake, shaking and sweating, cold yet hot at the same time. Even knowing that he was awake, it was hard to remember, difficult to think; prying open his eyes brought a blinding glare, and sent the world reeling.

Blinking, he held them open, forcing himself to remember, trying to piece things together, to sort out reality from dreams. Rain beat against his face—a steady downpour—and the light was no more than a gray haze. He was lying on the ground, not under a wagon or wrapped in his blanket, nor sheltered by a tarp—lying with one side of his face pillowed in mud, vicious, needle-like mud. Gradually he sensed that the prickling came from short, broken grass, dry and cured from the previous summer, still stiff even when wet.

To move was an effort. His muscles seemed chained, and the strength on which he prided himself gone. Water was at the edge of his mouth. As he moved again, he realized that his cheek was not only pillowed in mud, but his face lay half in a pool of collected rain water.

To sit upright was a monumental task. He steadied himself, shoving hands against the mud, until the slash of dizziness subsided. Looking about, he forced his mind to assess the situation. The half-light, dimmed by rain, suggested dawn; daylight was making a tardy arrival, water being wrung from the cloud blanket in dismal splashes. Shivering, he got unsteadily to his feet.

The sense of disaster was like a bad taste in his mouth. He looked about hopefully, but there was nothing to see. That was the trouble—the lack either of men or animals.

The chuck wagon, with its patched canvas cover, should be standing with the air of an uneasy steer, and Slim Bledsoe should be struggling to fix breakfast, complaining volubly at the vagaries of the weather. Off by the water hole, the big herd should be stirring to the activities of a new day, steers heaving erect with an air of surprise, cows beginning to graze, calves bawling in the loneliest of dawn sounds.

There was none of that; only the prairie, empty to the rain. Cal raised a hand to his head. As he suspected, there was reason for the pain there. His fingers came away smeared with half-dried blood. The sight of it brought full remembrance. Judging by the blood, as well as the ache, he must have served as target for a bullet; at the least, the slug from a forty-five had creased, rather than caressed, in passing.

The type of injury probably accounted for him being

alive. Had the bullet gone an extra inch to one side, it would have missed him; but an equal distance the other way would have placed it fatally. Still, he was alive, instead of buzzard bait, as someone had intended. Time, aided by the rain, had revived him; yet he must have lain unconscious through most of the night.

He had been awakened out of sound sleep. There had been confusion, a melee of sound, shouts and the crash of guns; he'd jumped to his feet, turning toward the source of the turmoil. He remembered a half-moon in the sky along with the feel of rain, a distant flash of what might have been lightning instead of guns, all confused now. There had been a dark wave of running animals, the shaking thunder of racing hoofs. There memory stopped, so the bullet must have set its period.

The silence of the dawn, the emptiness in place of stir, was the worst. His hand fumbled toward his holster and came away empty. Frowning to discover the cause, he saw that more than his gun was gone. Cartridge belt and holster as well had been stripped from him while he lay unconscious. Bleeding and unstirring, the attackers must have supposed him dead.

Such an error was reasonable, just as what had happened was clear. Cattle thieves had raided during the night, and had gotten away with the herd. Whether they were led by Strang, or might be a separate gang, he could only conjecture at the moment. As he'd warned Tom, he had glimpsed watchers during recent days—skulkers who were unwilling to show themselves as honest men would do.

His warning had only made the trio more stubborn, and this was the result. When they had refused to set an extra watch, he'd missed half his own sleep, trying to patrol. Three nights of it had dragged him down, so that he'd slept heavily—on the night when they had decided to strike.

Whether it was one set of outlaws or another, it was not surprising. The new railroad was bringing benefits to the border, and could be expected to bring others. At the same time, it was an added invitation to lawlessness; many a herd, being shipped to market, was loaded and sold by men whose only claim to the cattle was a bill of sale given by Judge Colt. Entire trail crews were occasionally wiped out.

Something of that sort had happened here. A man lay, face down, in the wet grass. Cal's head throbbed more sharply as he bent for a closer look, then straightened, feeling sick.

It was Sam Tucker. A bullet had taken him in the chest, then had come out at his back. The gouging size of the wound suggested that it had been fired from a buffalo gun. Tucker's belt and revolver had also been taken, his personal possessions callously pawed over. A quarter-plug of chewing tobacco, soggy from the rain, lay discarded.

Moving in a widening circle, Cal found a second dead man: Slim Bledsoe, the cook. This attack had been particularly brutal.

The ruts where the wagon wheels had stood indicated how it must have happened. Apparently Bledsoe had rolled out from under the wagon, probably half-asleep, confused. As he sighted along an old army pistol, someone had slipped up behind him, catching up the axe with which firewood had been chopped. The axe wound rivaled that of the buffalo gun.

The army pistol, still loaded, was partly hidden in the grass. Either it had been overlooked in the darkness or else the raiders had not considered it worth taking.

Cal made a wider circle, finding no others. Counting himself, there had been eleven men in the crew. Where were the others?

It was unusual for raiders in this strip of country to take any prisoners, but apparently that had been done. If Strang was back of this, then Tom, Tim, and True might be useful as hostages. That would not apply to the others, however—to Gil Jenkins, Big George or Dude Ellsworth, Limpy and Blaircom.

The manner in which the raid had been conducted, as well as its total success, struck Cal as the queerest part. The evidence indicated that the attack had been a nearly complete surprise. Tucker, Bledsoe, and he had tried to fight back, but had been cut down without a chance.

But what of the others? The Three Tough T's, the remainder of the crew? Not everyone could be surprised in such fashion—unless part of the crew was leagued with the raiders. That could make the difference.

That no real resistance had been offered was too obvious to overlook. The herd was gone, along with the horse remuda, the chuck wagon, everything that was movable. The completeness of the take-over stank of treachery.

Four of the crew were new to him. Big George and Limpy did their work in a manner to cause no complaint, but he had never warmed up to them. They cracked no jokes, indulged in no pranks or good-natured horseplay, even about the campfire after a day's work. They had been on Muleshoe before he came, but never of it.

Dude Ellsworth and Blaircom had been hired at the start of the drive. Since the Three seemed satisfied with them, Cal had offered no comment, but he had been surprised at the choice. Blaircom was the coldest-eyed man he'd ever seen, and the closest-mouthed. In a land where half the people were chary regarding their history and antecedents, he stood out as doubly secretive. But Tom had professed to be satisfied with his work.

Dude was by nature a dandy. An artisan in leather had

labored long to carve his saddle, and the rest of his outfit matched; he topped it with a pearl-handled gun. And though the Three had only contempt for a white-handled gun, no one had made light either of Dude or his gun. Perhaps that was the answer.

Those four might well have been members of a rustler outfit, seduced by the promise of gold, or planted among the crew in advance. That left only Gil Jenkins, and his absence troubled Cal more than all the rest. Gil had sent him that letter, had warned him of what was planned when the herd pulled out. He and Gil had eaten the dust of the drag all across Texas, red dust, gray and black; they had ridden night herd under the stars.

Because Gil was openly his friend, he had not been in good standing with the others. But Gil's absence was just one more of several mysteries.

Cal made a wider circle as the day brightened, but there were only the two bodies. The sign of the herd led on north, the roused cattle having milled about for a while before being lined out. Their tracks in the mud showed fresh, scarcely washed by the rain. Everything of value had been taken, and that could complicate the matter of existence in a land where everyone was potentially an enemy.

A sulking coyote attracted his attention, and he found a dead cow lying behind a clump of brush; apparently it had gotten in the way of a stray bullet.

They had not bothered to take his pocket knife, and Slim Bledsoe always carried a flint. Cal found that, also counted as worthless for loot. Now he could build a fire. Everything was soaked, but the rain was ending, the sun trying to break across the horizon. It would take a day to dry grass or wood; but there was usually some which remained dry if you knew where to look.

His head still ached, but there was a job to do, so he set about it. Where brush grew at the edge of a draw, he found wood dry enough to take a spark. Working with flint and steel, it was a chore to start a fire, but finally he managed. Ordinarily he was choosy as to his meat, but survival was the first rule. He cut a steak and broiled it.

The raiders had discarded a broken-handled shovel which Slim had kept in the chuck wagon. He dug a grave and, because it was shallow, he piled stones above it; those would guard against wolves of the four-legged variety. Another menace he could only risk. This was the edge of The Nations—a lawless land in every sense of the word. White men, the offscourings of the armies of both North and South, ranged here, their numbers periodically renewed by recruits, men who did not fit well in an ordered society.

Bands of red men claimed the country for their own, prowling in much the same fashion. In McCale's estimation, they were preferable to the whites. But you never knew quite what to expect. They might be friendly or hostile, depending on circumstances. Some might violate a grave in search of scalps.

Not much had been accomplished when the day was done. Even so slight an injury as the bullet crease was a sap to strength, and Cal stumbled as he moved. He made another meal, then slept, well back and away from where the fire had lifted its beacon of smoke.

By the next morning, the wolves had finished the meat. Worse, his appetite had returned. But a man could live off the land. By now, the herd, with its new guardians, should be a safe distance ahead. He set out, following the fading sign toward the north.

There were three chores to be done. The first was to mete out justice to the slayers of his friends, Slim and

Sam, who had died loyally at their posts. Next in line were his brothers, though he was not sure that they would welcome help if it came from him.

The final objective was to recover the herd. He needed those cattle to stock his range on the Yellowstone.

Never had the land appeared wider or emptier. Because of the rain, there was no dust, no cloud against the horizon to denote the progress of the trail bunch; he was alone in endless distance. The horizon had a trick of receding, to match and mock the plodding pace of a man. Not even a grasshopper disturbed the silence.

Cal felt most the lack of a horse, though on foot he could more than match the pace of the herd. In that aspect, there was time enough. Kansas, and the railroad—which undoubtedly would be their destination, as it had been Tom's—was still a long way off.

At midday he sighted a speck against the horizon; gradually it took form as a horse; then he saw that a man was on its back. Something was wrong. The pony would advance, then pause. More than once it changed course, apparently wandering as it pleased. As he drew close enough to see how the rider slumped in the saddle, the erratic conduct was understandable. The man was sick or injured.

With recognition, he was not sure whether this was good luck or bad. The horse had belonged to his own string, a rangy roan with the tireless attributes of the cayuse. It made no effort to veer away, but greeted him with a whicker of relief; the man who sagged in the saddle was Gil Jenkins.

Jenkins was unconscious, his hands gripping the saddle horn with a set desperation. The knotted bridle reins were looped above the horn, so that the pony was unable to lower its head to graze. Jenkins' breath was shallow and rasping. Blood, almost but not quite dry, made a stain high up on his back, by the right shoulder.

Water was an essential if Jenkins was to survive or even revive. From this point, for the first time that day, a straggly line of willows relieved the monotony. It was a couple of miles to them, slow miles, leading the horse. But behind the brush, a creek wound sluggishly.

Cal dropped the reins, allowing the pony to drink, then eased Jenkins down. Now he was able to obtain a better look, and he shook his head. The bullet had passed clear through the injured man. Such power could only be from a rifle; the miracle was that Jenkins had survived this long.

Cal washed his face, getting a swallow or so of water into his mouth. Jenkins coughed, then his eyes opened. He drank thirstily as water was held to his lips, and the vacancy in his eyes was replaced by recognition. The pleased shadow of a smile flickered in his eyes.

"Cal!" he croaked. "Where'd you come from? Those sons of guns told me you was sure enough dead."

"Looks like you and me both fooled somebody," Cal returned. "You better rest while I fix you up, Gil. Talking could be hard on you."

"I've got things to say," Jenkins insisted. "And it won't—make no difference. I'm sure—glad I found you. You were right—the other day. I overheard you arguin' with those stubborn chumps, warnin' them we should keep a sharper watch and double the night guard. Well, you know how we were jumped."

"Yes. They got me before I could get started."

"Happened that way all around, I guess. The dirty part was that we didn't have a chance, on account of being double-crossed right in our own camp. Man to man, we could have stood them off. I was ridin' night herd, and the first I knew that anything was wrong, I heard a shot off on the far side. I started to swing that way, when who should speak from right beside me but Blaircom. He'd sneaked up like a fox on a hen.''

Anger lent Jenkins strength. Since he was determined, and it could make no real difference, Cal let him talk.

'' 'You hear anything, Gil?' Blaircom asks, innocent as all get-out, and for just a second, he had me fooled.

'' 'I heard a shot,' I told him, and he says, 'Like this?' and ears back the hammer on his gun, with its barrel right in my face. 'Look behind you,' he adds, and when I did, there was Limpy, with another gun on me.

"By then, guns started popping like corn, but I was caught for fair. Blaircom told me he was doing me a special favor, 'stead of shooting me outright, like he might have done. He said I could throw in with the gang and get my share of the profits, 'stead of having the coyotes pick my bones. It wasn't exactly a matter for argument—and by then, it was all over with, anyhow.''

He choked, and his eyes screwed shut. Then he opened them and drank again, gaspingly.

"They aim to take the herd to the railroad in Kansas and sell them. Big George and Dude were in with them—from the start—and there's a dozen more. 'Course, they're pretty mad at your brothers, Strang in particular, after the way he was double-crossed.''

"Can't say that I blame him much.''

"Nope, it was a dirty deal—but like I told you before, they figured he'd double-crossed them to start it all. I wouldn't know about that, though I wouldn't put it past him, them being tarred with such a stick . . .''

"Them? Who do you mean?''

Jenkins' wandering attention came back, as with faint surprise.

"Why, I mean Strang and his pards. I finally got it fixed in my mind who he really was, after they jumped us. I'd seen him—a couple of times. He used to go by the name of Longstreth, during the war—Devil Longstreth . . ."

McCale needed no more to understand. Longstreth's Raiders had been a name to strike terror all up and down the Kansas-Missouri border. Technically, they were a part of the forces of the Confederacy; actually, like some others, they had been guerillas, pillaging and murdering without much distinction, as much feared and hated by the South as the North.

"I didn't let on like I knew him, for they'd have slit my throat," Jenkins added. "And to give the devil his due, I reckon he'd have settled for the ranch and let it go at that, if it hadn't been for that trick of havin' the nesters take over and leave them holding the sack. Right then, Strang and his friends decided for sure that it was all a put-up job so that your brothers could get away with those diamonds . . ."

"You're doing too much talking, Gil," Cal warned again.

"Makes no difference, I tell you. They've been insistin' that the Three dig up that sack, or tell them where it's hid. It's sure a devil of a mess."

"You mean those jewels are the real thing?"

"Must be," Jenkins conceded. "Loot taken from some poor devil in one of those raids—and I guess Strang bet them on the level. But Tom was ragin' mad, sure they were junk, that he'd been made a fool of, and he threw the sack away. Later, they all three tried to find the stuff again, but it never turned up. Now, Strang figures they're lying, that they've got the stuff cached somewhere. And he aims to make them tell where!"

That explained why they had been taken alive and were being held as hostages. Such conduct was not the normal pattern; but if Strang became convinced that the jewels had really been lost . . .

Events had evolved into a strange set of circumstances, which were logical enough when the backgrounds of the men involved were considered. McCale could even understand Strang and his way of thinking. Before the war, Longstreth had been a gentleman born and raised, but a man hounded by the law, with which he could never quite get along. The war had offered unique opportunities for both revenge and plunder, and had given him a fearsome reputation, but not a handy one once peace returned.

In the era following, it had become expedient to assume a new name and identity, and he had compromised. The life of a gambler tallied with the nature of Longstreth, but as a gambler, he had tried to maintain himself as a gentleman, to wear the cloak of respectability.

Now that phase of life had also been left behind as he was goaded to desperation and outlawry by the twisted chain of circumstances. Blundering as usual, the Three T's had enmeshed themselves in a deadly net.

"I pretended to go along," Jenkins added. "Till this morning. Then I made a break . . ."

The remainder of his story came in broken snatches. He had been overtaken within a few miles. Because the land was flat and open, there had been no place to hide, no cover from which to fight. All that he could do was trust to the speed of his horse, hoping, in a running battle, to match bullet for bullet.

"Only trouble was—a Winchester sure outranges a Colt's. I couldn't even slow them down—and a bullet knocked me right off my horse."

He had lain a while, unconscious. Finally reviving, he had found his horse grazing nearby. There had been no sign of the others.

"Reckon they figured me for dead—and even if I wasn't they knew I'd never get back. Likely they turned back when I went down, to save ridin' an extra mile."

Weak and dazed, but with one purpose firmly in mind, he had managed to pull himself back into the saddle.

"Somehow I—figured that somebody'd—be coming. Maybe a man—gets second sight—when he's so close to being over the hill. And I—hoped that maybe some of our bunch—could have survived. I wanted to—to help. Now I guess I—won't be able to. They're—a tough outfit . . ."

His voice trailed to a whisper and was finished. This time, water at his lips had no effect.

McCale shook his head. The lost diamonds altered the whole matter. If they had been lost, then the lives of Tom, Tim, and True hung by a slender thread indeed. Unless they realized that and managed to feed the doubt in Strang's mind, instead of persisting in the story that the stones were lost, he would soon lose patience.

## Chapter V

Both on a basis of friendship and what he had done, Gil Jenkins deserved a decent burial. The trouble was that now there was not even a broken-handled shovel with which to dig; but after some searching, McCale found a section of creek bank undercut by the water at flood stage. That had receded, leaving a slope newly grassed. Jumping up and down, taking a couple of spills in the process, he caved the bank down and contrived a passable resting place.

He owed Jenkins an additional debt, for the horse, a gun with ammunition, and a sack full of supplies. There was a chunk of bacon, a bag of dry beans, and other items which the deserting puncher had been able to grab. Included in the pack were matches, and these Cal welcomed most.

He felt a sense of loneliness such as had never oppressed him before; Gil Jenkins had been his only real friend in this part of the country. As he did several times each day, he wondered what had become of the Dulanes, but the land was wide. It would be better luck than he deserved or hoped for if he ever cut their trail again.

With the night, he rode north; it was ever more vital to go as unobtrusively as a shadow. The callous brutality of the three killings fanned his anger, so that he was compelled to battle a raging impatience to catch up, to come to grips. But time was his ally, and he must use it to the full.

He doubted that his brothers were in any immediate danger. Strang wanted two things from them, and one at least he could be sure of—a bill of sale for the cattle, permitting them to be loaded onto railroad cars and sold without any embarrassing questions asked. But that would not be needed until they reached the line of steel.

A bold stroke, which would free the prisoners and recover the herd at the same time, was what he wanted; the problem was how to work such a thing. Until he made a move, Cal would have the advantage of surprise, and he didn't want to waste such an asset. A single bad move could spell ruin.

Often, in the past, he had been impatient with the trio of older men, disgruntled at their attitude; nonetheless—and this was something they had never guessed—they had loomed in his boyish eyes as heroic figures, and some of that feeling remained.

Bad weather had plagued them for much of the way across Texas—rain, raw cold, howling gales; now, as though repenting of the harshness of its treatment, nature smiled with warm sun. It still lacked the heat which would scorch the land a little later in the season, but it was perfect for moving a herd.

Following his custom, McCale rode mostly by night, sleeping by day with his horse hidden in a draw or coulee. The land looked empty, but such an appearance could be at once an illusion and a delusion.

The trail freshened again, and he sighted the dust where the herd moved. After they had camped for the evening, he had a better look, from a vantage point of broken ground, no more than half a mile away.

The three had been riding, but among a group twice their number. That meant that they were closely watched, and any break for freedom would be met with a bullet. Apparently they had accepted the situation thus far; it was the reasonable thing to do.

Once the camp had grown silent, Cal went on foot, moving carefully. The outlaws had surprised them without much difficulty, and the same thing could be done again. Unless sentries were posted, an alert watch was impossible.

Then, as he saw the sleepers, he was forced reluctantly to concede that they didn't need a watch. The Three T's were together, Tim in the middle, his head to the others' feet, both wrists manacled. One handcuff was linked to True's ankle, the other fastened to Tom's. Prisoned in such fashion, they could make no break, not even walking or crawling.

Any attempt to free them of the manacles would rouse the camp. Cal considered the alternative—getting the drop on the sleepers, rousing them, and forcing them to release the three. But scattered as widely as they were, they would be impossible to control.

*From the looks of things, you three will just have to go on being their guests a while longer,* he thought. *So we'll do the next best thing, and give the others something to worry about.*

He watched the pair who rode night herd. Big George was one. They circled the cattle by easy stages, riding in opposite directions, singing in not unmusical voices. He moved to intercept Big George at the point farthest from the camp, while the other rider was at the apex of the circle. Brush afforded a cover, and he emerged from that and was alongside, face shadowed by his hat. His revolver barrel was lined across the saddle horn.

" 'Evening, George," he greeted. "I've a question for you. Would you rather kick in a noose or die by a bullet?"

The question, as he had intended, was disconcerting.

Big George goggled, eyeing the revolver in fascination. "Uh—I—I ain't partial to either," he confessed. "W-who're you?"

"I thought you'd remember me," Cal chided. "After this, you will—providing you remember anything."

"Cal McCale!" George gasped.

"So you haven't forgotten me—or the way you shot me from behind and left me for dead?"

The accusation was pure guesswork, but Big George's repeated gasp showed that he had been close. "It—it wasn't me," George protested. "Blaircom tended to that. I—I just happened to be riding with him . . ."

"There's an old rule in law that an accessory to murder is guilty, along with whoever pulls the trigger," McCale reminded him. "A matter of intent. And then you double-crossed some others who were supposed to be your friends. Slim Bledsoe was a mighty good cook. He deserved better than to die the way he did."

This time, Big George made no betraying answer, but he looked extremely unhappy. Cal reached across and helped himself to the outlaw's gun. "Let's keep riding," he suggested. "Then we'll talk some more."

Once a comfortable distance lay between them and the camp, Cal pulled alongside. By now, an alarm had probably been sounded, but there would be no hunt for the missing man during the darker hours of the night. He doubted that any would be conducted at all; men like Strang used traitors for their own purposes, but a turncoat was always despised.

"You have anything you'd like to say?" Cal asked.

Big George started nervously. "You—you ain't aimin' to kill me, are you?"

"Why shouldn't I? Do you deserve any better treatment than you gave others? With you out of the way, I'll have one less to bother about."

"Well—uh—if that's what's botherin' you, just let me go. I'll keep riding, clear out of the country."

Cal's laugh was contemptuous. "You'd swing around and join Strang again as fast as you could."

"Do you think I'm that big a fool?" George asked earnestly. "I wouldn't be popular if I came back. You can trust me."

"What are they aiming to do about my brothers?"

"Nothing—if they show any sense. It's up to them."

It was clear that Big George could tell him nothing new. Cal gave him a taste of his own medicine, keeping him tied during the day, while he slept. Then, with his promise to ride the other way, he let him go, not caring too much whether he kept his word or not. If he carried word back, their uneasiness would be that much greater.

The next afternoon, they came to a stream which he judged to be the Canadian. And here was opportunity and temptation. The far shore showed rough and broken for miles. It was good country in which to hide, and better for ambush or bushwhack.

He could easily beat them to the river and across, and pick a vantage point. From that, a single man with a pair of guns could wreak havoc among the crew, once the herd was being pushed across. Tom, Tim, and True should be ready to take advantage of a break, and if they moved boldly, they might be in control again by the time the herd was over the river.

The trouble with such a plan was that its success depended on shooting without warning, killing as many as possible before they could reach shelter or a chance to fight back. And he knew, even as he considered the chance, that he couldn't take it.

His brothers would deride him for softness. The outlaws had not been deterred by qualms when killing was to their advantage. It was the logical move, and would afford a fitting revenge. But there was another hazard, not lightly to brush aside. Once they saw what was happening to them, and with no target at which to shoot back, they would turn their fire upon their hostages.

*So that's out,* he thought, not without relief. *But I'll get on across ahead of them, and see if something turns up.*

He was pleased to note that they rode now in pairs. That would be the result of Big George's disappearance, and for them, it meant extra work as well as uneasy nerves.

He circled, then crossed the river, miles upstream from where the cattle would reach it. Circling back along the far shore, he shook his head in wonder. This was truly a place for ambush. The southern bank was wide and the water shallow, but on the north the bluffs rose sharp and formidable. Deep, swift current churned close to bhe banks, which at most points were sheer and unclimbable.

One man could certainly make it unpleasant for even a big crew, and with little risk to himself. But there was another reason why such a vendetta would be self-defeating: with guns blasting at them, and no riders to guide them to the only decent landing, the cattle would swing back, panic-stricken, milling wildly. Half the herd could easily be lost within minutes. Like it or not, he had to keep this crew alive, to keep moving the herd toward its ultimate destination.

But there should be more opportunities for harassment, for such action as he had used against Big George. Fear, especially of the unknown, could lay the nerves of a crew ragged.

Distance, in such country, was usually deceiving. Even the cattle felt the trick as the day wore on and their thirst became a plague, and the river took on the appearance of a mirage, coming no nearer. Finally, they were almost running, but the afternoon was waning before they reached it and began to drink. A pair of riders circled the mass of the herd and pushed on to test the crossing and scout the unfriendly-appearing northern slope.

McCale watched from his vantage point. Dude Ellsworth seemed to be in charge now, and he headed unswervingly for the one spot where cattle or horses could gain a foothold on the bank. A score of places appeared equally inviting, but deep water, savage currents, or other obstacles made them a mockery.

"That's the trail, Mr. Strang," he said confidently. "Looks like a blind alley, but it opens up to an easy beach—though the path's not much wider than a wagon road. I helped take a herd across here last year."

It proved out as Dude described it, and they came splashing ashore, Strang peering uneasily at the towering walls on either hand, where the trail led back from the river, climbing and twisting for nearly a quarter of a mile before breaking into the open. There was plenty of evidence that it had been used on numerous occasions, but the grisly possibilities were suggested by the bleached bones of a horse, and, farther along, a human skull.

"It's a fine crossing," Strang conceded dryly. "And the devil of a spot for ambush, if anybody should feel like jumping us!"

"Sure is," Dude agreed. "I guess there's been a lot of blood stainin' the river here, one time and another. But if there's a better crossing within a day's drive either way, nobody's ever found it."

That, of course, was the deciding factor. McCale granted them courage as they explored, watching particularly for any sign of recent occupancy. He debated whether he should jump them, and decided against it. If Strang failed to return, his brothers would be given a rough time.

They made only a cursory inspection before turning

back; a rock-to-rock, hole-to-hole hunt, along the breaks, up and down stream, was out of the question.

As soon as they returned to where the crew waited, the chuck wagon drew off and preparations were made for the evening meal. McCale watched in surprise, though he could understand Strang's reason. They were violating a cardinal rule of the trail. Always, when you came to a river, you crossed without delay; you did not wait for a new day, even if darkness was already encroaching, and no matter how tired men and animals might be.

The reasoning behind such a course was sound. A new day might prove perfect, but it could just as easily bring new problems. A sudden storm upstream during the night, with a wide watershed spilling into the river, could turn a placid creek into a raging, impassable torrent. Another risk was that enemies might arrive, to challenge the crossing.

As old a campaigner as Strang knew all the hazards, but he was choosing to wait. Cal suspected that this was an indirect tribute to himself. If there were members of a rival crew of rustlers hiding along this bank, or only himself, Strang probably had plans for finding out. But that could be a double-barreled game.

Sounds, such as the bawling of cattle, came muted across the water. The cook fire blazed brightly, sank to a glow, and vanished. Presently, to the accompaniment of faint splashing, figures emerged ghostily from the river and moved up the trail. There were four of them. Two turned upstream, where the trail widened, two went down. They rode in pairs, not risking it alone.

An hour later, the splashing was repeated; but only two re-entered the river and crossed back. When the others failed to appear, Cal knew that they were waiting, watching for anyone who might move on this side.

"Just so I know." He nodded, and grinned to himself. "I won't let it spoil my sleep."

The beat of rain and the smash of thunder awakened him. The rain proved to be only a mild spatter, and most of the thunder was a long way off. It might be something for Strang to worry about, but not himself.

Daylight justified his midnight guess. The river was a sheet of turbulence. This was what experienced guides warned against as a price of delay, either for wagons or trail herds. Somewhere upstream, the storm had been heavy; now the run-off was tumbling over itself in a sort of frenzied exuberance. Mud sullied the evening's clear silver, and driftwood bounced on the crest. The water along the southern bank had spread back for at least a quarter of a mile, where the slope was easy.

The camp had been hastily moved back to higher ground. Cal could picture such a job, while the river rushed them in heavy darkness, but at least they had managed. A new cook fire burned beside the chuck wagon, and there was no sign of distress. The herd, farther back, grazed comfortably.

This would mean a day's delay, but time was no objective; the high water would render crossing today too hazardous.

It was a lazy day on the far side of the river, while the cattle grazed and rested, and men washed garments or slept in their turn. McCale did not yield to the temptation to relax in similar fashion, certain that he was not alone on this side. Vigilance could be tiring, and when it had to be continuous, without moving, it was doubly a strain.

If the pair were really there, they were doing a good job, revealing no sign of their presence. Sooner or later, such a tiring wait must result in carelessness. By early afternoon, the water was starting to fall, though not to a point where a crossing was advisable.

Sundown splashed like a bloody gash across the west when Cal saw the first movement. A hundred feet upstream from where he sat, a man edged up the face of the bluff. He might almost have passed for a beaver or otter—possibly a coyote or puma—prowling the river bank, so well did he blend with the background and so carefully did he move. But something caught the last rays of sun along that open bank, a betraying glint impossible with any animal.

Since the flashes were directed to the far shore, most of them were invisible from this side; but the watcher was flashing with a bit of mirror—apparently a signal to the camp that the way was clear.

He finished as the sun seemed to be put out in the river, and began to descend. And in that moment a horror of unleashed fury swirled about the spy and engulfed him.

## Chapter VI

There was little to see in the swiftly gathering night, and less to hear; but the silent, swarming ferocity of attack was not to be mistaken. It was Indians who pulled down the victim, doing it so quickly that he had no chance for either outcry or resistance.

A second flurry, equally fierce and just as brief, erupted from another hidden spot nearby; the second man had been set upon, probably as he sensed the danger too late and tried to go to his companion's assistance.

McCale waited, feeling a prickling of danger, and now his straining ears brought new sounds, muted but distinct—a soft breathing, the stroke of a hoof against a stone, the uneasy switch of a horse's tail.

The sound came from an unshod hoof, and to senses trained in such intangibles, the difference was readily apparent. About to move, Cal froze with his back to the cliff, breath in check. He was thankful for the swiftly closing darkness, now filling the gulch like a deepening pool of ink. The newcomers were making use of the same cover, but moving boldly, sure that they were in full control of the situation. And the dark would hide any betraying sign he might have made. Even if some should be found, they would probably attribute it to the other pair.

Judging by the sounds, many men rode in this company, pressing to the river so that their ponies might drink. He needed no closer look to sense the danger of this crew. The overlong wait by the river had brought its inevitable peril in this country—Indians.

Lawless white men roved in bands across The Nations, sometimes leagued in an uneasy truce with the original red settlers, more often hostile. Such a truce, where it existed, could rarely be trusted; harassed increasingly by the encroaching waves of settlers, along a hundred tangents of the frontier, many tribes of red men were finding The Nations a last but uneasy refuge.

Observing the banded outlaws, some of the red men were taking lessons from their book, occasionally emulating them, wtth certain refinements of their own. Generally they took vengeance upon all whites whenever the opportunity offered.

A single man like McCale—or even a small crew—might ride for days with only a nominal risk of detection, since the country was so vast; but a big trail herd could not be hidden. The dust of their passage was like a pillar of cloud by day, but it was not a symbol of protection.

It was probable that scouts had been keeping an eye upon the herd, for most of its passage thus far into forbidden territory. So long as the cattle moved steadily, shepherded by a big, gun-handy crew, the Indians kept off, respecting their rights. But the flooded river and the extra day's delay had not been lost upon the watchers. Clearly, they had been hoping for just such an opportunity as was now presented. They intended to make use of the facilities, offered by this crossing.

Their advance scouts had detected the watchers when they moved, but they had waited until the all-clear signal had been flashed before they struck. Nothing would have been seen or heard on the far side of the river.

Horses were allowed to drink, following what had probably been a long, hard ride to reach this place in time. Then they came back, crowding the narrow gulch, dismounting, eating cold food, resting, talking in muted tones. Listening closely, McCale decided that they must be Arapahoes.

'Pahoes, Cheyennes, Sioux, Crow, Pawnee, Apache —all these and more ranged this strip at one time or another. Ancient rivalries had been mostly submerged, by an unwritten but tacit agreement. Mostly they kept out of one another's way, concentrating their fury against the white invaders. Sometimes they co-operated.

Right now, they were as sleek and contented as cats. They had a fresh pair of scalps, taken without risk, and the stage was set for a massacre to their liking.

Most of the warriors carried rifles. In the night, it was impossible to judge whether these were muzzle-loaders, smooth-bores, or possibly modern guns; but nonetheless, they were guns. He estimated that at least half a hundred men were crowded in here. The ponies had been led back, out of the way; the braves remained. That gave them odds of three or four to one, by comparison with the unsuspecting crew across the river.

They might wait here for the cattle to cross the next day, striking devastatingly from ambush. That would be the way with white men, but Cal doubted that such a method would suit them; they would probably cross during the night, striking without warning. In such an attack, they could probably attain their primary objective, of making off with the herd. In the course of the attack, they would cripple the trail wolves to a point where they would be unable to attack in turn or retake the cattle.

McCale held motionless, barely breathing. His patience had outlasted that of the spies planted by Strang, and their bad luck had saved him—so far. But the Indians were all around him, and there was no way to turn without moving among and through them, no chance to slip away without exciting suspicion. They had come so fast and silently that he had been trapped before he knew it.

The one good part was that they didn't know it, and in the heavy gloom here at the bottom of the canyon, it would take a keen pair of eyes to discover any differences. Some people liked to claim that an Indian could tell a white man by the sense of smell, and Cal didn't doubt that; he could do the same. There was a gamy, unwashed odor to the band, compounded of fetid breath from eating entrails and raw or half-cooked meats—fare which whites regarded with disfavor. Part of the odor came from crouching winter-long above smoky fires in close-drawn tepees, until they were smoked and cured like hams. The stench was a common denominator of the band. Under similar conditions, white men would smell the same.

But the lack of such odor would hardly tickle the nostrils. A couple of men were close enough to that he could have touched them without moving. They squatted about, hunkered on their haunches, patiently waiting for the time to strike. Once the camp across the river was soundly asleep, they would be in for as rude an awakening as they in turn had inflicted upon the original trail crew. Had it not been for his brothers, and the added fact that he owned an interest in the herd, Cal admitted, this would be poetic justice, grimly written in red.

All talking subsided. Patience could be a virtue, and

Indians knew how to practice it when a reward was in sight. Some shifted position, and with backs to the walls, appeared to doze. McCale was not deceived; such naps were as light as those of a cat.

Waiting, under such conditions, was a strain; but so far, luck had been with him. The night before, he had concealed his own horse in a small grove of trees, well back from the river. There was grass enough and water from a small spring, and he was pretty certain that neither the pair of spies nor the Indians had discovered it. If his cayuse had heard the Indian ponies, it gave no betraying neigh. Horses, like men, acquired an instinct in such matters. A trained cow pony was almost as leery of an Indian horse as of other wild animals.

The night was changing. The rim of the river showed now, a lighter hue than the surrounding gloom. Something moved at the edge of the water—the sinuous shape of a mink, progressing upriver, and, like all of its kind, as insatiably curious as it was hungry. It poised, a forefoot lifted, back curved like a tight spring, testing the air with eyes and nostrils. The eyes made tiny green sparks. All at once it was swallowed by the water, as silently as it had come.

An Indian commented, amused. Others answered, voices low, but interested. Men stirred and shifted to more comfortable positions. The incident was a break in the monotony; it seemed that everyone had been awake and seen the mink.

The moon was moving in a long stalk across the sky. It would soon be overhead, able to look into the canyon, to shed light in dark places. McCale watched the retreating shadows uneasily. He was certain that the others knew where he was, just as he knew about them. So far, they had not grown suspicious, despite his silence. Some men were always taciturn, and they respected that right. But his skin, under the light, would show betrayingly.

Another quarter of an hour and the first rays would pick him out. To move would be to attract attention. There was light enough now to add to his worry. Every Indian was bare-headed. He had suspected that, but had not been sure. For some time, he had been sitting on his own hat, to keep it out of view.

The hatbrim would conceal his white skin, but he dared not wear it, since none of the others had hats. He could make a jump and run for it, and if he did that now, he'd have the advantage of surprise. That would get him possibly half the way to the river, to a fighting chance; by then, they'd swarm him down.

He could give a good account of himself while it lasted, with guns spitting, but the only advantage would be that the sleepers in camp across the river would hear the guns and be warned. As a last resort, he'd do it that way, but he could see no advantage to hastening the inevitable. It would spell the end of a hopeless, all but impossible dream—of finding Carrie again. And it might terminate her own dreams. He had no way of knowing about that, but a man could always hope—at least so long as he was alive.

His nerves were getting ragged; he almost jumped as one man got to his feet. He stood a moment, as though listening, then grunted a word of command. There was prompt response, the stir of activity. McCale's hope that some would move up-canyon was spoiled; instead, the horse tenders came moving down it, bringing the ponies. The cayuses were without saddles, twisted rawhide thongs around lower jaws serving for bridles.

A horse was given him, along with the men on either side. So far, they accepted him as one of the band. Cal grasped the rein and swung quickly on to the pony's back, as the others started to mount, before it could detect his strangeness or shy away. If it went into a vicious cycle of resistance, bucking and plunging, he'd be undone. He had no doubt of his ability to ride the animal, but the others would be quick to sense the wrongness.

The foremost men were riding into the river. The motion saved him, as his pony moved with the rest. The fingers of his right hand, clutching at the mane, felt the dry sweat which caked its coat. The war party must have ridden fast and far, through the day and right up to the hour of darkness. The weariness of the pony was his own salvation.

Back on shore there was some confusion. One warrior was finding himself short-changed, without a mount; but it was too late to delve into such a matter, and it was being solved, temporarily, by the extra man riding double.

As if to make amends for its earlier curiosity, the moon ducked behind a drift of coud. Almost at once they were in deep water, the ponies forced to swim. McCale slipped off, as the others were doing, swimming alongside, holding to his pony's tail, allowing it to tow him. With his other hand he managed to hold his gun above the water, as the others also were doing.

Then, in most cases with an ease and smoothness to rival that of a swimming mink, they were climbing back on, as the water shallowed. It was time to make a move, to veer away from the main body of horsemen, to sound the alarm. A warning to the outlaws was only self-preservation, both for the herd and for his brothers. Roused before the Indians could strike, the rustlers would give a good account of themselves. In a battle on fairly even terms, both forces might be seriously decimated. That was what he had to play for.

Strang, faced with a sudden attack, would probably

unlock his prisoners and give them guns. Whether they would be able to take advantage of the situation then was up to them, a matter of luck and possible skill.

The moon came out as suddenly as it had vanished, a sheen across the water. The turbulence of the previous night was missing, the flood one more episode in the river's long history, not even its memory disturbing the placidity of the current. Only the mud flat ahead waited like a morass.

Another man had been riding alongside. He turned and started to say something, and Cal saw the change in his face, the darkness which came over his eyes. He moved fast, a hand darting, lifting, holding the gleam of silver. A long-bladed knife at close quarters could be not only silent but deadly.

Apparently he had no doubt concerning his speed or skill, but the knife was still in his hand as McCale's revolver shattered the silence. The warrior spilled from his pony and into the water in one long motion, and Cal forced his own mount to a sharp turn downstream. The cayuse resisted, fighting the change, knowing its rider alien, but he swung it around and headed back for the shore they had left.

The gun triggered pandemonium. There was a shocked instant of silence, during which surprise all but paralyzed the group. Then, seeing what had happened, realizing that their surprise was spoiled, they vented their feelings in a wild series of yells. The horses plunged ahead to the attack, though a couple of men who were near enough turned their attention to the renegade in their midst.

A second shot checked the nearer one. The other warrior's pony went into a fit of panic, as the shadows swept back across the water. Taking advantage of the cover, McCale forced his horse into the deeper current, but this time he stayed on its back; by the time it scrambled out on dry ground, the battle on the opposite shore had joined.

The warning of the shots had not been lost on the white men, and the enraged whoops of the 'Pahoes had told them what to expect. One thing could be said for Strang's wolves: They were swift to react in the face of peril. A volley of blasting guns blunted the charge. The night covered the resultant fury.

## Chapter VII

Thoroughly weary, McCale slipped from the pony, allowing it to run, then, working well back from the river and the canyon trail, he found a hidden cove where it would be safe to rest. He had warned the whites, and that was as much as he could manage; the rest was up to them. Judging by the sounds, he estimated that they had done all right.

The Arapahoes, disgruntled and enraged at their failure, would be coming back, and they would be looking for him. But the moon was gone now, the darkness heavy. He doubted that they would stay around until daybreak, for by then, the herd would probably cross; and after one repulse, it wasn't Indian nature to plan a second, different sort of attack. They simply thought in different fashion from white men, and did things in different ways.

When he awakened, fully alert, caution held him without movement. For the moment, as he opened his eyes, he could see nothing. Dawn was in the air; on the higher ground above the river it had pushed back the night, crowding it into pockets, in coulees and temporary refuges under brush or trees. Here it was making a final stand, the gray like a layer of fog.

His ears brought a stealthy scrape of boot on rock. As he

turned his head, shock coursed like a dash of snow against the face. The muzzle of a gun was leveled a scant couple of steps away. Behind the gun, his face sardonic, was Blaircom.

McCale's former estimate—that Blaircom was the coldest-faced man he'd ever seen—appeared fully justified now. He'd had, he guessed, probably four hours' sleep; hours in which the renegades, as well as the red men, had been wakeful and on the prowl. Some of the outlaws, as well as the Indians, had been looking for him. And that, too, was understandable; the fact that he'd saved them by sounding a warning wouldn't impress them with any feeling for gratitude.

Blaircom, as he'd seen demonstrated in target exhibitions along the trail, was fast with a gun, and deadly in accuracy. His greatest asset in such a contest was a lack of scruple. He would shoot a man with no more compunction than a coyote, and had bragged of doing so.

"Go ahead," he invited now, his voice dry. "Make a try, if you want to."

"Can't say that I do," McCale admitted. "The only thing I'm curious about is, how you found me?"

Blaircom's chuckle held no humor. "I got to wondering about those warning shots, and who could have fired them. Fact is, I've done a lot of wondering, lately. Like about who was stickin' on our trail, like a burr to a horse's tail. I decided that it was likely you, and that whoever it was would be off here, waiting it out. That would be the way I'd do it, a case like that. So—with the 'Pahoes drawin' off to lick their wounds, I risked a ride across."

"That still don't explain how you found me. Or was it luck?"

"Luck?" Blaircom's dry laugh grated. "Mister, there ain't no such thing as luck. A man makes his own—one way or another."

Cal didn't argue the matter. To disagree with Blaircom would hasten his pull on the trigger.

"Nope, luck didn't have a thing to do with my findin' you," Blaircom assured him. "I knew you'd be hangin' around over here, and I'd pretty well made up my mind about where. So I did some looking, and here you were. You picked a good hidey-hole—but you made one bad mistake. Mighty bad."

He waited, and when McCale failed to oblige him by asking what that might be, he grunted triumphantly. "You snored!"

"That was sure a dumb thing to do," Cal conceded. "The only trouble is, a man don't have much control of such things when he's asleep."

"I'll fix that so it won't bother you any more," Blaircom assured him. "And so you won't hinder *us* no more, either."

"You figure that it was a hindrance, my giving you warning before the Indians were on top of you?"

"Well, no." Blaircom pondered the matter as though attempting to be judicious. "That was a good turn, right enough, but I don't figure that you really deserve any credit for it. You were thinkin' of your own scalp—and mebby the hair on those ornery brothers of yours. What you wanted was for us and the Injuns to fight each other to a standstill, which we pretty well did. That leaves you standin' to profit. And of course you'd keep on stickin' your nose in our affairs—which we can't allow."

"It was pretty much of a draw, then, the fight?" Cal was considering his chances, and finding them poor. If he made a move, Blaircom would shoot; but so long as he could keep the outlaw talking, there was always a possibility.

"We lost two men killed, and a couple more was hurt. Leaves us short-handed, but there'll be bigger shares for the rest of us. I figure we downed at least twice as many of the 'Pahoes, though it's hard to be sure, for they take their dead when they pull back. I reckon they had enough. Not," he added honestly, "that we required any more our own selves."

"You took a risk, crossing the river to hunt for me. They'll be on the prowl."

"Aw, they've cut and run. I ain't so big a fool as to risk my hair—not till I know what I'm doing."

That was not intended as boasting, merely as a statement of fact. Blaircom had traveled a risky trail so long that self-preservation had become a matter of instinct. While they talked, the grayness had thinned. A splash of salmon along the east heralded the march of the sun.

"We've palavered long enough," Blaircom added. His tone changed from reasonableness to a growl. "There's nothing personal in this, you understand. Fact is, Kid, back in Texas, I kind of sympathized with you, the way those three treated you like you was a fool. Which was a mistake on their part. You're smart, so I can't afford that sort of a mistake. That's why I'm givin' you a lead pill for breakfast."

## Chapter VIII

The blasting gun jerked taut nerves, even though he'd been expecting it. It took a moment to realize that he was unhurt, that the bullet had come, not from Blaircom's big forty-five, but from another, more ancient weapon.

Blaircom stood, in the brightening light of sudden sunshine, with a startled look overspreading his face. For the first time in years the mask of hardness slipped, revealing bewilderment and hurt, as on a small boy's. He made a valiant effort to hold his own weapon steady, to squeeze the trigger, but the task was beyond him.

All at once his fingers and his face went loose, and the gun slipped to the ground. As his legs buckled, he pitched half across the gun, and one fist clawed at the dirt.

McCale came erect, gun in hand. Blaircom had probably tried to make certain that the Indians had pulled out, after the failure of their surprise attack. Certainly they had retreated, according to their own mode of warfare. That was one great difference between red men and white. If a fight proved too costly, an Indian considered it good sense to quit, instead of attempting to prove his courage, by keeping on against heavy odds; he was bothered by no false standards which might impel suicidal conduct.

In the darkness and confusion, both the Arapahoes and Blaircom had overlooked something. One of their number had been missed and left behind, badly wounded. How he had gotten back to this side of the river didn't matter; perhaps he had seen Blaircom steal away from camp, and had made a supreme effort to follow. There had probably been riderless horses running loose.

Perhaps he had profited in turn by Blaircom's mistake. As the outlaw had pointed out, a snore could be heard a long way in the silence; but so could a man talking.

In the Indian's mind there had been no differentiation between the two white men. Both were enemies who had played havoc with the plans of the 'Pahoes. Leaving his horse, he had crept up while Blaircom talked. Hurt as he was, it had been a chore to raise his gun, an almost insurmountable task. But he'd gotten off his shot when he could bring the gun to bear.

His plan had included both whites, turning the gun from one to the other, making a clean sweep. He worked as desperately as Blaircom had sought to at the last, and his effort turned out to be as futile. Already, he'd exerted himself to the limit, and his strength was gone. The gun muzzle tipped to point downward, and he could not bring it up again. He fell forward, from his half-crouch, almost beside his victim.

The brace of shots had been heard across the river. McCale noted the sudden stir in the camp. Following the repulse, the camp had quieted, and weary men were probably trying to snatch a few additional winks. But roused and uneasy, some might cross to investigate this latest development.

It was time to move, before they arrived. Keeping out of sight, McCale got to his own horse, which seemed happy to see him. All the grass within reach had been close-cropped. He mounted and headed upriver, taking advantage of rocky ground, of every piece of available cover. It quickly became apparent that he'd have need for it, as well as some of the luck at which the outlaw had scoffed.

A passel of riders crossed the river and, finding the dead men, took up his trail. They would deduce that the Indian had killed Blaircom, but that made no difference; an enemy was on the loose, and they were in the mood to eliminate him.

Cal was not particularly worried.

He doubled and twisted, a game reasonably to his liking. If they kept coming, he could whittle down the odds against him still further. The drawback to such a course was that he needed these men so they could keep driving the herd, at least as far as Kansas. To continue depleting their ranks at this point was to risk losing everything; there were other rustlers who would be eager to take over, as well as other bands of angry Indians.

From a vantage point, he observed that his pursuers had split into separate groups. McCale chose his spot, then waited as a pair came in sight. One was Limpy; his companion appeared to be one of the original rustlers.

He allowed them to ride past, then stepped from behind and called sharply. Caught at a disadvantage, they whirled to stare, making halfhearted grabs for their guns, then thinking better of the matter as the sun slanted along the barrel lined in their faces.

"I'm giving you a choice," McCale informed them, "and a chance to live beyond the span you deserve. Like I say, it's up to you. You can still reach for your guns or grab a handful of sky."

They sat a moment, considering, not much tempted. Limpy spat and raised his arms.

Cal disarmed them, then made them dismount. They

obeyed, watching him uneasily, fully aware of their own untenable position. But for his warning shots in the night, they would probably have been overwhelmed while they slept. He'd had a stake in saving them, but they could recognize that he'd run a big risk in doing it. To hunt him in return, as they were doing, was base ingratitude.

"You going to gun us the way you did Blaircom?" Limpy snarled.

McCale looked at him and declined to reply. Limpy had been a friend of Blaircom, and, like him, he prided himself on his toughness; but he had the grace to color, knowing how Blaircom had really died.

Limpy's companion was not of heroic mold. Knowing how they would have treated him if given the chance, he was visibly quaking. "Give us a chance and we'll do anything you say," he pleaded. "Maybe you need some help. You can count on us."

"I can count on my fingers, too, and I'd get farther that way," Cal returned dryly. "I see that you have a knife. Take your lariat and cut it into several lengths. That's something you *can* do."

His command was executed promptly. Limpy watched in open scorn, but refrained from comment as Cal ordered the other man to tie Limpy's hands behind his back. But his zealous desire to please brought a growl of protest as the cord was jerked painfully tight.

"You're doing all right," Cal approved. "Now climb back on your own horse. With your hands together, in front of you."

Taking one of the lengths of rope, he slipped a noose over the outheld wrists, jerked it tight, then tied a knot and fastened the rope's end to the saddle horn. That left the rider the use of his fingers. Another length of rope was passed under the horse, and Cal used the ends to tie his prisoner's feet.

Limpy watched stoically, but his uneasiness cracked the mask of indifference when Cal took Limpy's lariat, opening the noose, and settled it in place over Limpy's head. The loose end he tied to the other saddle horn, beside the bound hands of the outlaw.

Their faces might have been sprinkled with flour. Cal judged that they would tell the truth, at least as far as they knew it. "How are my brothers being treated?" he asked.

"Fine," the second man assured him hastily. "Strang aims to take good care of them."

"On account of the jewels?"

Limpy shrugged, then seemed to regret the gesture as the rough strands of rope rubbed against his throat. "Them, among other things. Though he's getting right impatient with the way they try to keep stalling."

"They still kept handcuffed every night?"

"How else would you keep a bunch like them?" Limpy countered. "We treat them as good as they'll let us, but they sure ain't what you'd call co-operative. Last night, Tom sure cussed Strang out for not turnin' them loose to try and fight off the Indians."

Cal could feel no particular sympathy for either side in this dilemma; both groups were at fault and they had brought it upon themselves. But at least the trio appeared to be in no immediate danger. He'd help them as much as he could, however.

"You fellows are lucky that I have some use for you," he informed them. "I want to send word to Strang. Make it clear that I can play just as mean as you fellows do—if I find it necessary. If Strang gets rough, so will I."

"You going to take this special fittin' necktie off me now?" Limpy asked.

"No. I figure you need it to remind you of your shortcomings. Your friend will guide the horse, and you'll walk behind, at the end of that rope. I don't think you'll have to swim the river. They'll be coming across, so it shouldn't be more than a few miles till you join up with them."

Limpy's usually ruddy face looked blotched and flabby. "You mean I have to keep up or have my neck cracked?" he squalled. "What if I should stumble? I wouldn't have a chance."

"More of a chance than you gave Sam and Slim," Cal reminded him. "You should have thought of such things before selling out."

He mounted, leading the extra horse, and rode out of sight. Neither man, after that last reminder, had anything more to say; such treatment would infuriate the trail wolves, but it might teach them respect. The Three T's would know that he was working in their behalf. They should be able to plan their conduct accordingly.

Better mounted, and with extra guns, he was in improved shape to weather what might lie ahead. That was well, for he had a feeling that the opposition would become increasingly rough. But at least it worked both ways. So long as he kept out of sight, like a mosquito buzzing in the dark, the outlaws would sweat. Even riding as a team they had not been safe, and that sort of uncertainty would gnaw at them.

Instead of keeping on, he concealed the horses, then climbed to a vantage point and watched as the herd crossed the river. It gave him a certain grim pleasure to observe the precautions which they took until the cattle were out from the breaks, into open country again. Limpy and his guide joined them. Significantly, their plight failed to set the crew off on a fresh search for himself.

He could always tell where the herd moved, and estimate with reasonable accuracy how many of the crew were with it, or away on business which might be concerned with himself. By contrast, they had no way of knowing where he might be—whether ahead or behind—or what he might do. It was fox and hounds in reverse.

It was still a long way to the railroad, where the line of steel was shoving west, changing a nation as surely as the thrust of a blade into flesh. In some ways, as he'd observed on his journey to Texas, the likeness was apt; its penetration was as red with blood, but from the wound would come healing, and a change even beyond the dreams of the road builders.

The immediate dislocation was great, the problems of the railroad increased sharply by the urgency with which drovers sought to use it before it was really ready for any such volume of business. Homesteaders would follow before long, the tide spreading out on either side of the tracks, but they had not kept up with the westward thrust. In between, as in The Nations, was a sort of no man's land, a savage vacuum.

McCale still had no certain plan for dealing with the outlaws, once Kansas was reached, or for gaining control of the herd. He was counting heavily on his brothers, when the time came. Otherwise, it would be his word, or even theirs, against the crew; and no one would be impressed, even if they believed them.

There was no law in that part of Kansas to which he might turn for aid. An occasional town, plagued beyond endurance, hired its own marshal; but such men had no authority beyond the reach of their guns.

It might be well to stay behind a while, to let Strang and his partners stew in uncertainty. There was always the chance of others taking a hand, other outlaws or Indians, the possibility of a break.

He camped for three days beside a small stream, reveling in leisure. When that palled, he went on. The country seemed wilder, more lonesome, empty even of the big herd. Only the sign of their passing relieved it from utter wildness.

Strang was pushing farther to the west than most trail herds—whether from ignorance or with some purpose in mind, Cal could only speculate. By pushing his horses, he could overtake them within a few hours. Knowing that, he jogged easily, perversely choosing to ride by day again. The sun had passed its crest when he saw smoke.

Nothing in this land could be more alien than smoke at midday. At morning or evening, the infrequent wanderers of a wasteland halted to cook, but never at noon. Smoke in the middle of the day could be seen too far, too betrayingly. Yet the smoke was there, a wispy curl, twisting like a question mark. Cal swung toward it, riding with increased caution, but as his view improved, the caution seemed unnecessary.

A black blur scarred the surrounding green, and from it the smoke was fading. Someone had ventured into forbidden territory, building a cabin, perhaps a homestead shack. Unlikely as it seemed, there were always a few people brash enough and hopeful enough to venture far beyond the border. To Cal's mind, they were the real pioneers, braving hazards greater than those faced by the trapper or prospector, cowboy or hunter. They marked their place with a house, and tied themselves to the land, sacrificing freedom of movement.

Such hearty souls changed a continent more surely even than the makers of a steel road. After a few false starts and needless sacrifices, the home-builders took over, and the frontier receded like a mirage. But the firstcomers almost always paid a price; their monuments were as brief and ethereal as the smoke which marked the end of hope, along with the destruction of tangible property.

The country lay silent, empty; not even a scavenger circled in the sky, though the lack was no indication of safety. Cal dismounted. This fire must have blazed at dawn. The ground was cooling, ashes stirring in the breeze. As he started to circle, a voice shocked him to immobility.

"Stop where you are! Stand or I'll shoot!"

## Chapter IX

McCale turned slowly, careful to make no false move; his eyes searched the landscape, momentarily baffled. There was a break—a gulch—a short distance away, and brushed fringed its edge. The leaves were unscorched by the fire. There was probably a spring there, to furnish water for whoever had tried to build in this place.

On the opposite side from the burnt spot was more brush, no higher than his knees. Then he saw the snout of a gun barrel poking up from the earth, and began to understand.

This was wide-open country, here in the last unclaimed, untamed wedge between states—country rare as the day, with so little breeze that the smoke could climb untrammeled. Usually the wind pushed tirelessly, as though a thousand miles of space was not enough. On occasion, it turned wild and savage, twisting freakishly on a mad romp. Twice, McCale had sighted tornadoes, then had seen the destruction after they had passed; he'd seen a cow snatched and carried over a barn, a blade of grass driven through a plank.

Whoever had settled here had risked the roving bands of Indians, the worst scourge of outlaws, the winter blizzards or summer sun. But he had prudently dug a storm cellar for protection against the twisting wind, roofing it so that it was all but invisible. And today someone had survived in the cellar.

The door was open a crack, the rifle barrel poking through, lined on him. Though that was surprising, it was the voice which amazed him. It held an edge of roughness, firmed desperately against overriding nervousness. But for all its quality of command, it was unmistakably the voice of a woman.

Cal stood a moment, unmoving. Then, gravely, he doffed his hat.

"Ma'am," he said. "I don't know what's happened —though I can guess. I saw the smoke and rode to have a look. You don't need to be afraid. I'm a friend."

Silence hung like haze in the air between, as though his words were being weighed, considered against the immensity of what was and what had been or might be. The gun barrel wavered, cutting a small arc. Then the door of the storm cellar heaved open, and the sun glinted along the rifle barrel, no longer pointed toward him, but held with hands whose grip whitened the skin at the knuckles with a dreadful intensity.

"Cal!" Her voice was incredulous, disbelieving, rising from a whisper to hope, to joyous welcome. "Oh, Cal, it can't be you!"

Surprise held him for an equally incredulous moment, then he was moving forward, arms outstretched. Today she wore a man's blue jeans and shirt, instead of a dress, jeans which revealed a glimpse of trim ankles as she climbed from the cellar. It was what he'd dreamed of and hoped for, but almost too much to believe in; this was Carrie, whom he'd rescued from the little town misnamed Plentywood, on his way to Texas.

"Carrie! My dear!" He had her in his arms, feeling the warmth and softness of her, but also how she trembled, shuddering convulsively as she clung to him, her head buried against his chest. The wonder and the tragedy smote him as he began to understand.

This was the place which Cash Dulane had chosen, seeking room in which to breathe, country where the smoke fire of the nearest neighbor could never stain the skyline. That part of his ambition had been fulfilled, for no lonelier spot existed even in The Nations; but trouble had found them here, even as in a town.

"Carrie, honey!" His voice broke. "Oh, Carrie, am I glad to have found you again! I've hoped for this—though not this way, only to find you. I've kicked myself a thousand times for ever letting you go!"

She looked up at that shyly, eyes bright with tears, yet a touch of color was returning to pallid cheeks. She seemed satisfied with what she saw and heard. A sigh escaped her, but not entirely from sadness.

"Oh, Cal, I—I've wished it, too—and hoped that you'd find me again," she confided, then she colored and buried her face against his chest again. Looking down, he was startled to see that her bright hair was hacked and ragged.

"What have you done to your hair?" he demanded.

She started, smiling uncertainly, reaching to feel of the hair with tentative fingers. "I—I tried to cut it. I hoped that—dressed this way—that no one might notice that I—I'm not a man."

He guessed that she had slashed at her tresses with a knife, rather than trimming with scissors. It had been shortened, but the effect was unconvincing. Cal hid a smile as he studied her.

"Well, maybe—if you had a hat to cover it," he conceded. "Though you're most too pretty to be anything but a woman. But what's happened?"

Carrie's eyes strayed to his horses, now grazing with

dragging reins. They clouded as she looked about, then returned, searching his face in a desperate quest for reassurance. She nestled closer to him.

"Oh, Cal, like Ma s-said—our prayers are answered, for I've been praying that you'd find us again. I don't think I could have lived if you hadn't come. This was the place that Pa fixed for us. We got here a couple of weeks ago. It was pretty hard going. I guess Pa was hurt a lot worse by that fall from the wagon than any of us thought at first. He kept getting worse. Not all at once or very fast, or maybe we could have turned back. Ma and I didn't know what to do. And, the way it was, there wasn't much that we could."

Cal nodded understandingly. Dulane had seemed to be all right, but when a man took a fall and lay so long unconscious, serious aftereffects sometimes resulted.

"This morning, I got up early, to hunt. We—we were pretty short of food, with Pa sick and everything. I was off two or three miles when that big trail herd came along. I suppose they must have camped not very far away last night, though we didn't know about them. When I looked back this way, the cattle were milling all around the house."

McCale nodded. "I know about the herd," he explained. "They belong to my brothers and me, and we were driving them north when a gang of trail wolves jumped us one night and got away with the cattle."

"Stole your herd? How dreadful. But you called them trail wolves, and that's what they are. I was too far away to see much or to hear what went on, only there was shooting. Pa hadn't been himself lately. When he was able to do anything he was nervous and jumpy. Likely he tried to stand them off with a gun . . ."

She drew a deep breath, then went on slowly:

"When I heard the shooting, Cal, I—I was awfully

frightened. I hid out in the brush until they went on. There were so many of them. I—I guess I'm pretty cowardly."

Cal nodded with grim understanding. One mistake had probably led to another, one shot, followed by a fusillade, before anyone really understood the situation.

"You did the only sensible thing, after what had already happened," he reassured her. "It was too late to make any difference, and some of that bunch are not only trigger-happy but downright vicious."

"I—I would have come, anyway, only there was smoke, right after the shooting, and then fire. By the time they went on, the house was burning all over. I came as soon as I dared after they'd gone. Pa and Ma were b-both dead." She pointed to the patch of brush. "They're over there. I dragged them away from the fire and into the brush—to hide them from wolves or v-vultures. I was trying to dig a g-grave when I saw you coming. I thought it was one of them coming back, so I hid in the storm cellar."

Aside from the unnecessary tragedy of the day, Cal found none of the story particularly surprising. Cash Dulane, as he'd gathered at their other meeting, was one of the horde of well-meaning men who could never quite adjust to reality. Though he undoubtedly loved his wife and daughter, he had never been a family man—only a foot-loose son of the frontier, an impractical dreamer.

Haunted by the responsibility which he usually managed to dodge, he'd compromised by building a cabin here at the edge of nowhere, then going after his family. The odds, heavy against the success of such an undertaking, had grown steadily worse after his injury.

Carrie had had part of the day in which to work and plan, spurred by desperation. It had been clear to her that she could not remain here. Yet to try and journey anywhere on foot had been almost as appalling a prospect.

The raiders had helped themselves to the wagon and team, and whatever else seemed worth taking.

Yet, since travel she must, she had planned to go as a man. She had donned a pair of jeans and a shirt which her father had left in the storm cellar, and which the raiders had overlooked. Then she had tried to hack off her long, betraying woman's hair. Though she did not say so, Cal knew that she had been on the verge of despair.

Cal crossed to look at the dead. Both had been shot several times, apparently in a panicky fusillade. Dulane might have brought it on by a nervous shot to begin with; still, it was brutal and senseless.

Carrie had her rifle, but nothing else remained, except a spade in the storm cellar. Unaccustomed to its use, she had not accomplished much, particularly in such a distraught mood.

"I think we'd better place them in the storm cellar, and cave some of it down over them," Cal suggested. "That will work better—and there's no other need for it now."

Carrie nodded. "That will be all right. I didn't think of doing it that way. I—I guess I haven't been thinking very straight."

"Considering all that's happened, *I* think you've done all right," Cal commended her. "Just what did you plan afterward?"

Her smooth little jaw set stubbornly. "I aimed to overtake them—and make them pay for what they did!"

"Then we're in just about the same boat. They're holding my brothers as prisoners—more or less as hostages . . ."

"Your brothers? Oh, Cal, I didn't understand. That's awful!"

"It's not good," he admitted. "Though I guess it works out as more of a chore than they intended to take on. Those three can be a problem without half trying, and when they set their mind to it . . ." He grinned and shook his head.

"The rustlers intend to drive the herd to the railroad in Kansas, and either sell them there or ship them east to market. I aim to stop them—though, so far, I don't quite know how."

Carrie eyed him sympathetically. "I'm sorry, Cal," she said. "It's as bad for you as for me, isn't it? A while ago, I didn't see how things could be any worse. But maybe it could have been. Ma and I talked matters over, just yesterday, and we knew that Pa couldn't last much longer. Afterward—we were going to try and get back to Missouri, but I know we'd never have made it. Ma's cough had gotten a lot worse lately. Now, this way—she will be with Pa. That's what she really wanted."

Her words revealed more of heartbreak and tragedy than she knew, and Cal was tempted to take the horses and head straight for the ranch on the Yellowstone, to by-pass the herd and all that it represented. It would take longer to build up an outfit, but with Carrie beside him, he'd manage. And if things went wrong, in Kansas or anywhere along the way . . .

The trouble with that was threefold. Carrie had an interest in this as well as he did, there were his brothers to consider, and his own determination to have what belonged to him. McCale stubbornness, perhaps.

As though reading his thoughts, Carrie spoke gravely. "Don't worry about me, Cal. We'll work this, somehow. I can shoot as straight as any man—and if necessary, I will!"

He nodded. "I don't doubt that. This will take a lot of doing, but as you say, we'll manage."

They made a common grave, as he had suggested, and once the task was done, Carrie picked a handful of wild flowers for a final tribute. Reading the unspoken wish in her eyes, Cal said a prayer above the grave. It was halting, as uncertain as his tongue at such a task, but she seemed pleased.

He whetted his knife on his boot, then smoothed Carrie's hair as well as possible, feeling awe as he fingered it. He'd never realized that a woman's hair could be so silky.

"I guess it has to be done, since you had the job started." He sighed. "Still, it's a crime, spoiling hair like this."

"I knew that I couldn't fool anyone, with it so long," she returned. "Anyhow, it will grow out again."

They prepared a meal from his provisions, then set out. Cal explained his philosophy of the chase—that for the present it was a game of waiting, of harassment, keeping their enemies guessing. Then he changed the subject, telling her about the spread in Montana, the rich grass, stirred by summer winds, the beauty of the winter landscape. Some of his enthusiasm for the country crept into his voice, and he saw color return to her cheeks.

With Carrie riding beside him, the way he'd dreamed about for so many lonely weeks, he was conscious of a sense of excitement, of promise such as the future had heretofore lacked. He was tempted to remark that for him, this was a day of good luck. But as she glanced back for a last time to the black which stained the prairie, to the unmarked grave, he doffed his hat in tribute and kept his thoughts to himself.

## Chapter X

Now, more than ever, it was necessary to take precautions, to travel by night and rest by day. Two people and two horses could be seen more readily than one, and Carrie was a precious possession, to be protected. The land appeared as empty as it was wide, but eyes could watch unseen, and the only safe axiom was that every stranger should be regarded as an enemy, unless and until proved otherwise.

Cal chose the camp site with more than usual care, where a creek afforded both shelter and water. A deep, sluggish pool yielded double bounty. First he pulled some fish from it; then, as a muskrat swam past in the early light of dawn, he rapped it sharply with the end of his fish-pole, and drew it to shore. Roasted over a small, smokeless blaze, muskrat was good meat. He preferred to avoid using a gun in this silent land.

Carrie washed some clothes at the edge of the creek, spreading them among the brush to dry. When finally she prepared to get some sleep, with afternoon shadows lengthening, she called softly to Cal, where he lay at the far side of the embers from the cook fire.

"I—I'm saying a prayer of thanks for you, Cal—for you, and that you came just when I needed you most, both times. I—I don't know what I could have done, if you hadn't. I don't believe I could have managed."

He had trained himself to sleep by day, but it would be harder for Carrie until she grew accustomed to an inversion of pattern of light and dark. He was dozing when a sound awakened him, more disturbing as he recognized what it was. Carrie was crying, the soft sobbing a heartbroken sound.

He hesitated, then lay quiet. It was up to him to look after her, and he intended to do the best job he knew how. Part of that meant staying on his own side of the fire. In any case, there was not much to say, which could help. Words, at such a time, were light as wind.

He awoke as the moon arose, but waited another couple of hours. Carrie was sleeping heavily, exhausted from strain and grief, and there was no hurry. When at length she did awake, it was with the tantalizing fragrance of roasting fish in her nostrils. She sat up, looking bewildered for an instant, then, seeing his face in the small circle of firelight, smiled and came to her feet.

"Good morning, Cal," she said determinedly cheerful. "Or should I say good night? That doesn't sound right, either. But that smells good, and I'm hungry."

She went on, as they ate. "I was just thinking about the way things work out. How we met your brothers, back in Texas, and then you . . . and you found me again when—when it counted most. Lots of things seem to happen, more or less by accident, but I guess it's not so much accident after all. Your brothers were just like you, Cal—so friendly and helpful."

His face was expressionless as he placed more sticks on the blaze, but the words startled him. Somehow they were not the sort he'd associated with The Three Tough T's.

"They gave us so many things that we needed—shot and powder and all sorts of stuff which they insisted we'd need and they had no use for. It must be awfully hard on them, to be taken along as prisoners."

He had been thinking along those same lines; it was time to make another attempt to free them. It was possible that the vigilance of their guards might be relaxed after all this time.

"I think we'll catch up with them, then I'll sneak into camp and see if I can't find a way to get them loose."

Carrie nodded. 'If you can do that, then the five of us should be strong enough to do things. We can drive the herd, and stand the others off, if we have to. But how will you manage?"

That had bothered him for a long while. If they were handcuffed as before, there was just one possibility. "I guess I'll have to persuade Strang to unlock them," he said. "He must have the keys."

"Yes, we should be able to work it," Carrie agreed. "I suppose they've tried to keep watch and guard against something like that, every night. By this time they'll be tired, and pretty well off-guard. And they'll be watching for one person, not two."

"But you're not going into their camp with me," Cal insisted. "I can't allow that."

"But I could help," Carrie protested, then, finding him determinedly opposed, she made another suggestion. "All right, if you want to go alone, then you slip into the camp and I'll keep watch with my rifle. I'm a pretty good shot—and if anything starts to go wrong, I'll make sure that you have a chance to get away."

Though he hadn't thought along such lines, Cal was forced to agree that it was a good idea. A gun at his back would be a big plus factor.

Two nights later, they prepared to make the try. The herd was bedded down, the cattle mildly restless but not unduly so, the camp apparently asleep. There was less than a half-moon, hovering like a pale moth in the night sky. It gave some light, but not too much. Carrie chose a vantage point behind a fair-sized boulder, resting her rifle barrel across it; from there, she would watch his movements.

The men riding night-herd were well at the side, and if anyone else was on watch, Cal could detect no sign of it. His own experience with a trail herd had taught him how wearing it grew to be, especially after weeks of steady travel. You learned the art of sleeping in the saddle by day, dozing as you rode, but such snatches of rest were never enough. There were too many nights of storm, of stampede or restlessness on the part of the cattle, when it was impossible to sleep at all. Sleep became a sort of game which you played, an elusive something which you snatched on every possible occasion; it was a thing to be cherished, fragile, almost out of reach.

Alertness gradually gave way to weary resignation; that was probably the situation now. Increasingly shorthanded, due to the tolls of the trail, exhaustion permeating flesh to the marrow of the bones, men slept when they could, no longer mindful of risk. He heard the heavy snoring of men in deep sleep.

Taking his time, he moved cautiously, looking them over. The first thing was to locate his brothers, to judge what precautions to take. Men who slept by themselves could be disregarded. As always, the Three T's would be together.

The trouble was that they were not. He circled about, looking more carefully, able to recognize two or three of the sleeping men. One or two stirred, then went on snoring as before; still there was no sign of the three.

Uneasiness knotted his stomach. He'd counted on finding them readily enough, expecting the only real risk to come when he tried to free them. It hadn't occurred to him that they might not be there.

If he'd delayed too long in this try at helping, and if the outlaws had tired of bothering with them, had gotten rid of them . . . The possibility was too real to be dismissed, though he was in a cold sweat at the idea. He moved to the wagons, risking a look inside, under the canvas of each. There were two wagons, both of which were familiar. One was the Muleshoe chuck wagon, with which they had originally set out. The other had belonged to the Dulanes.

In one sense, his luck was good. No one had ridden in to call men for herd duty, and none of the sleepers had been disturbed as he prowled. But the wagons were like all the rest; they were empty of the trio he had come to find.

Dude Ellsworth was sleeping somewhat apart from the others. Like the rest, he was beginning to show the strain of the trail. His usually smooth shaven jaws were ragged with whiskers, grimy from lack of washing. Since he had to take somebody, Dude would be an excellent choice; he was the guide. Cal dropped to his knees beside him.

"Dude," he whispered. "Wake up!"

On the first days of the drive, Dude had been a light sleeper. Now it required shaking as well as insistent whispering to rouse him. He started to groan and turn, then checked, suddenly awake, at the cool pressure of a gun barrel against his temple. As his eyes widened, he saw the gun, with the hand which held it. His gaze sought to turn and follow the hand, along the arm, to the grim face looking at his.

"Come along," McCale instructed. "And easy does it, or this gun might go off!"

The breath went out of Dude in a long sigh, but he did not seem inclined to argue. He got to his feet, moving ahead as directed. Memory of Limpy, who had returned to the herd with a noose about his neck, of others who had vanished and had not returned, seemed to hold him in a sort of thrall.

They reached the boulder, and Carrie came out from its shadow and went along with them. Dude goggled at her in disbelief, but kept moving away from the camp. Not until they were beyond any possibility of being heard did Cal call a halt.

"Now let's have it," he said shortly. "What's happened? Where are my brothers?"

The Dude's answer was as surprising as all the rest. He shook his head. "All I know is, they rode away a couple of nights ago. Just got on their horses and left."

The knot which had been twisting ever tighter in Cal's stomach loosened a little, but this was hard to credit. "Do you expect me to believe that?" he demanded.

Dude shrugged. "Maybe not," he admitted, "but that's what happened. Strang let them go. I figure they made some sort of a deal, but I don't know. Nobody tells me about such things. All that I know is that they pulled out, and the rest of us were plenty glad to see them go. They were a problem to watch. Three or four times, they came mighty near turning the tables on us or getting away."

There was no good reason to doubt that he was telling the truth. Their absence would account, in part, for the lack of precautions about the camp. Knowing the trio, he could readily credit that they would have made as much trouble as they could contrive.

The incredible part was not merely that Strang should allow them to ride away, but that they would consent to go, except by escaping. There were elements here which he found increasingly disturbing.

"Did they have a gambling session with Strang and his partners, before they left?" Cal demanded.

"Come to think of it, I guess they did," Dude admitted. "I was riding herd, so I didn't see much, but from what little I heard, they must have had quite a game. What I couldn't figure was what they'd be playin' *for*. They didn't have anything to put up for stakes."

But in that he could be wrong; and Cal's relief was tempered by coldness as to what those stakes might have been.

## Chapter XI

Further questioning convinced them that Dude was telling the truth. In one way, what happened was both logical and understandable. The three had been uncooperative prisoners, and must indeed have been a problem, which the cattle thieves had been anxious to solve, by ridding themselves of them. Dude offered a possible clue.

"Strang and his pards did a lot of of arguing, about what to do with them. Along toward the last, and specially after that shootin' of a woman—nobody realized she *was* a woman, till it was too late—why, some of them were getting ugly. A few extra killings didn't seem to make much difference, and Limpy told Strang that he aimed to solve things by buryin' them. Only Strang wouldn't agree to that. He said he was no murderer, whereat Limpy retorted that he didn't need to worry on that account, he'd tend to it himself. But I figure it came to a showdown, and they worked it out with the cards."

That Tom, Tim, and True were alive and apparently free, was a relief. But they had gambled again, after loudly proclaiming that they were through with all such activities for good. Which must mean that the reason had been impelling. But what had they been able to put on the board? On one side, clearly enough, had been their lives.

But with those more or less forfeit to begin with, it would take a lot to counterbalance them, in the eyes of the rebels.

The missing jewels? That seemed unlikely. McCale was convinced that they had been telling the truth—that they had lost or discarded the supposedly bogus diamonds, and had no idea as to what had become of them.

There remained the herd, and his guess was that they must have relinquished their claim to ownership, in exchange for their lives. With death the alternative, he could not quarrel with their choice.

Never having been a gambler himself, Cal found some aspects of such a deal hard to understand. He knew, however that most gamblers—even tinhorns and cheats—kept their words religiously, once a deal had been decided by the cards. They might seek to manipulate the cards, or lie and cheat, and possibly murder; but they honored a gambling debt. And because of that, prisoners and captors had played a game, and they would both stick to the agreement.

For his brothers, that was well enough; but he himself had played no game, made no commitments. He still intended to have the herd back, since part of it belonged to him, and he needed it to stock his own range. But now the matter of getting possession of the cattle, and getting them to Montana, was, if anything, more complicated than ever.

"You'll ride along with us for a couple of days," he informed Dude. "After that, we'll turn you loose. You can do as you please, though if I was to make a suggestion, it might be wiser to stay clear of that bunch from now on."

"I aim to do just that, if you give me a chance," Dude agreed. "I wouldn't be popular with them after this—and I was getting pretty well fed up with the whole bunch, anyway. I sure made a fool of myself, going in with them in the first place. I guess I ain't cut out to be an outlaw."

On that plaintive note they parted company, two days later. They were in the Kansas country now, still wild and lonely, but in process of changing. Still, when they sighted a horseman, heading their way, Carrie grew shy and troubled.

"How—how shall I act?" she asked. "It's been so long, and I've met so few people, Cal—aside from you, that I don't rightly know how to behave when I meet anyone."

"I guess most people out in this country feel the same way," Cal reassured her. "When you meet someone, either they don't have a word to say, or they talk a streak, trying to make up for lost time. I remember a squaw man I met one time. He sure wanted to talk, but he'd lived so long among the Indians that he couldn't remember half the English words."

The rider showed no sign of veering off, but he came on with a certain wariness, since good intentions could not be taken for granted. Cal watched with the same intentness, somewhat reassured by the stranger's outfit. He might not be a tenderfoot, but he was certainly not too long from the country east of the river.

"Howdy, folks," he greeted, then, staring hard at Carrie, touched his hat. "Don't often meet anyone around here, these days," he added. "Not much like it was, half a year ago."

"What makes the difference?" Cal asked.

"The railroad, I reckon. You ever watch a little sort of a whirlwind movin' along the ground? It can sure pick things up and stir them around as it goes, but once it's passed, everything settles down again. It's been that way with the railroad. Brought a whole rush of things and people with it, but they all stay pretty much at the spot where the building's going on. Once they're gone, nobody stays behind. Except maybe a chump like me," he added mournfully. "I believed what they said about gettin' rich by homesteadin' a chunk of ground, and come out here and got stuck on a quarter-section of land, along with ninety-eight coyotes, nine hundred prairie-dogs, and this old nag I'm a-ridin'. And now I'm stuck for proper, with everybody else gone on."

Carrie smiled understandingly as she met Cal's eyes. Here was proof of garrulity, after long silence.

"You say the railroad is here—that it's built past this section?" Cal asked.

The settler waved an arm in general gesture to the north. "It's right over there, beyond those bluffs. Couple of miles and you'll see the rails. There and in business—such as it is." He indicated a faint smudge on the horizon. "There's a train now. Westbound."

"I—I've never seen a train!" Carrie confessed, excitedly.

"You ain't? Well—I guess you ain't missed much, at that. They sure ain't what they're played up to be. But come on, and we can see it as it passes. It'll be along in a minute."

He swung his horse, leading the way for a quarter of a mile, to the height which he termed the bluffs. From there, small with distance, they saw the train crawl into sight, smoke belching from the wide stack of the locomotive, then edge on past and vanish again. There were less than a score of cars. Its whistle echoed back, a long, lonely sound. The settler spat.

"Not much to it," he observed disparagingly. "Ain't never been much to it. I was led to believe this whole land'd be settled thick by now, with towns an' schools and such-like—but why'd anybody ever want to come here, 'less they was loco, like me? Wind and jackrabbits—I forgot the seventeen hundred of them long-legged critters. And they can run, only that there ain't nowhere to go."

"How many trains do they run?" Cal asked.

"One west one day, to the End of Steel, back again the next day—when they make it. Lookin' around here now, you wouldn't believe that we were right at end of steel, just a few months back with a town and everything. End of steel, yeah—and of just about anything that you might mention." A resigned smile lifted his mustaches. "Two thousand settlers—that's what they called them. They settled like grasshoppers, and left just as sudden as a swarm of them pesky critters. Now the coyotes scratch there by night. Not a soul left. Aside from a hundred or so that's restin' in Boothill, that is. The town went on when the steel did."

"Nothing to keep a town going, otherwise, I suppose?"

"Well, my business didn't seem to be enough to hold it." He snorted disgustedly. "I guess the railroad counted on a lot of haulin', one thing and another, but it's as scarce as snow in July. There are a few adventuresome dudes from the East, that ride out and look from the windows. Sometimes they poke out a gun, and take a shot at a buffalo or maybe an Indian. They see lots of emptiness, and take the next train back, and boast of how wild the country is, and dangerous. Other folks listen. And the flock of settlers that the railroad was hoping for, they decide they're lucky to be right where they are already. And which I can't blame them for that."

"It'll take time for them to change," Cal agreed. "Mostly they'll leave it to the cattlemen to tame the range before they start shoving. Are many cattle being shipped east by train?"

"Nope. There were quite a few, up till a few weeks ago. Seemed like you could see a cattle train, any day you looked. But that's most all finished. The market back there went all to pieces. Too many, I guess. Right now, longhorns don't pay enough to settle for their own ride."

He added, grinning, "You ride on a few miles west and you'll come to End of Steel again—and the town, which ain't much more'n the construction camp. And scattered around there you'll find half a hundred herds, all the way up from Texas. They're all cussin' the railroad, and everybody else they can think of, for the way things are going. Most everybody figured to ship east by rail, and make a pot of money. Now they don't know what to do or where to go, and all the time, more cattle keep coming up the trail. You got a spare four-bits, you can buy yourself a whole beefsteak on the hoof."

He was probably exaggerating, but such a turn, unexpected by the riders struggling up from Texas, might be good news for them. Cal explained, after they had ridden on.

"If the market back east is glutted as he says, and no one is shipping out, then Strang will find that he has a herd on his hands, and nothing to do with it. Which gives me an idea. He has a crew already. Maybe he'd take the herd on to Montana, for wages and a little spending money besides."

"Why wouldn't they look for land for themselves?" Carrie asked.

"It's not that simple," Cal explained. "There's plenty of range left, but lots of it is risky—even without the handicap of being outlaws. Like this country around here. There's good grass now, but by late summer, water holes from the rain and snow melt have all dried up. Springs and creeks are few and far apart. When winter comes, there's no shelter from the wind. A herd can start drifting with a storm, and when spring comes, they'll either be dead or clear out of the country."

"I guess I don't know much about cattle," Carrie said humbly.

"Well, a lot of folks who thought they did, have discovered that they had a lot to learn—trying to make a new start on strange range. But the word has been getting around, and it leaves a lot of men scared. Now, those who are held up here, will be fair caught on the horns of a dilemma. But it may be a break for us."

The line of the railroad grade still showed raw and new, the twin slivers of steel reflecting back the setting sun. Now the hazards of The Nations were behind, but at least those had been known and predictable. The sort they might encounter now could be worse.

"When we get to town, I'll get barbered to look halfway respectable, and then try finding Strang and making an offer," he explained. "I don't think there's anything to lose, for our feud can be more or less forgotten, now that my brothers are out of the deal, and the herd is here but of no use to them. Strang might jump at the chance."

He checked, listening, and the sound of hooves came louder, several riders jogging at a trot. They waited, wondering if the riders might pass without noticing them. There was no cover to withdraw to, only the gathering dusk. Soon it became apparent that they would be seen. Carrie's face was pale, and Cal's hand hovered close to his gun. From the voices, these were white men, but that was no guarantee of friendliness or integrity. Then Cal exclaimed, between surprise and relief:

"It's all right, Carrie. Sounds like my brothers!"

## Chapter XII

"What in tunket are *you* doing here—and with *this* little lady?" True demanded. It was by way of being a rhetorical question, covering some of their embarrassment at the encounter. Tom and Tim were staring, still speechless.

"I suppose the answer to that is that we're traveling, the same as you are." Cal shrugged. His first sensation of relief at finding them again, free and in good health, as Dude had said, was giving way to puzzlement. Their attitude had always angered and bewildered him, but never so much as now. He was glad to see them, and conditions being as they were, he had expected as much in turn. But apparently such a development was too much ever to expect from them.

"I don't quite understand this." Tom dismounted, and doffed his hat as he turned to Carrie, but his voice was gruff. "We're mighty happy to see you, ma'am—Miss Carrie—to find you alive and all right. Uh—after the way things happened, there at your place—of course we recognized your folks, after it was too late—and we were sure afraid of what might have happened to you."

"Trouble was, we didn't dare say anything to that bunch, fear it'd make it that much worse," Tim added. "It was kind of a mistake on their part, to start with, but that didn't help none."

"I was off hunting at the time," Carrie explained. "I don't know what might have happened to me afterward if Cal hadn't come along when he did. It was pretty awful."

"It sure was, and we were fair sick about it," Tom sighed. "It was a piece of luck that you were away. But we've been haunted, thinking about you."

Their concern for her was not only genuine but warming, revealing a side which Cal had seldom seen. He grinned at them. "Meeting you now takes a big load off our minds, too. We've been worried about you."

"Oh, yeah? Well, you sure didn't show it," Tom returned acidly. "Leavin' us to be treated worse'n the cattle."

It was Carrie's turn for a burst of temper. "And just what did you expect Cal to do?" she demanded. "You refused to listen to him or be on guard against trouble, so were caught when there was no reason for it, in the first place! And he was shot and left for dead, afoot, and with no supplies! That was the position he was in! And he did try to rescue you. But when he went into the camp and tried to get you out, you weren't there!"

"You mean to say he really tried—that he risked going right into their camp, after us?" Tim sounded unbelieving.

"He certainly did, and he brought Dude back out, as a prisoner! Dude told us that you were gone. But you three owe him an apology, for even thinking such a thing."

True answered, unexpectedly humble.

"After what you've told us, I guess we do," he admitted, then went on in a greater burst of frankness. "We've known for quite a while that we made fools of ourselves, refusin' to pay attention when he warned us of trouble. And I reckon if he hadn't kept plaguin' Strang, that gang might have killed us as the easy way to be rid of us."

"Dude said you gambled with them for your freedom," Cal suggested. "That so?"

True nodded. "Our lives and freedom," he confirmed. A rare grin twisted h s face. "That's one time we were lucky."

"Well, I'm glad it worked," Cal assured them. "What do you say if we all forget the past and start fresh? I suppose you've learned, as we have, that nobody is shipping stock east, with the market the way it is. That makes a difference for Strang, as well as for us. Working together, we can prove ownership, get the cattle, and go on to Montana. By the time they're ready for market, we'll be in good shape all around."

Again, to his bewilderment, there was no show of enthusiasm on their part. The three eyed each other after the manner of small boys caught in mischief.

"Yeah, I guess the market back east is gone," Tom said finally. "But I'm afraid we can't do it that way. Not after the—the way things have worked out."

"Do you mean you won't help?" Carrie asked incredulously. "Not even to get your own herd back? Why, what sort of men are you, anyhow?"

Tom shuffled unhappily, and blurted a confession which Cal had never expected to hear from his lips. "Since you ask that, Miss Carrie, why, I reckon we don't amount to much. Not near so much as we've liked to try and make ourselves think we did. And I don't blame you—or Cal—for feeling put out at us."

"I expect you must have some reason, Tom," Cal suggested. "Mind telling us what?"

"Just this. Strang's whole crew got might jumpy nerves, with men disappearing, or being made fools of, the way you did with Limpy and his sidekick. And Strang was as jumpy as any of them. He didn't know what to do, but his partners wanted to solve things by doing away with us. They'd kept us that long, figuring we had cached those diamonds and rubies somewhere, and could be made to tell. But if the damn jewels were real, they sure fooled me. I don't know what ever became of them. So—when they got to believing that, too, there was a lot of quarreling over us. Strang offered to settle it by playing us a game of cards—our lives against the herd. We didn't have much choice."

Cal listened with increasing respect. He had never quite understood these three older men, any more than they had him, and he doubted if he ever would. But at least they lived by their code.

"We won," Tom added. "Which gave us the right to ride away. But of course we had to have something to put on the board, and Strang named that—the herd. So we had to give him a bill of sale for it. After that, we can't very well try to take it back."

There was a scattering of small boulders here, and Carrie sat down on one of them abruptly. Cal had the same sensation of being let down. For a little while it had seemed that the big problem was solved, that they could go as a team, enlisting the support of other law-abiding men, and so recover the herd, probably without firing a shot. Now, to be told that they had been signed away . . .

Not that he could blame the Three. Strang would have carried out his threat, had they refused the gamble. That it had automatically been stacked so that he won and they lost, no matter which way the cards fell, seemed to have escaped them.

"I don't blame you," he said wearily. "It was the thing to do under those circumstances. Only there's another side to it. A share of that herd belongs to me—and I didn't make any agreement. Besides, the whole herd was stolen to start with, which pretty well rules out any such agreements made under duress. I aim to have the herd back!"

For almost the first time that he could remember, he caught a gleam of admiration in their glances. True sighed. "Well, more power to you, Cal. Seems like we've let you down, and ain't no help at all. Best thing we can do is ride on and not be a hindrance. Like you say, you ain't bound by what we did."

"You try that, you'll get yourself killed for nothing," Tim snapped. He seemed upset.

"That's my risk," Cal returned woodenly. "I'll take it."

All at once, there seemed nothing more to say. They turned, and saddle leather creaked as they swung back on to their horses. The brief hope of understanding seemed to have faded with the suddenness of the reunion. Carrie watched in silence, obviously troubled and disappointed. Then, as they started to ride on, Tom turned for a last word.

"We let you down, Kid," he said, "but not quite all the way. I had one thing in mind, which I didn't mention. That bill of sale that we gave ain't worth the paper it's written on. You'd turned twenty-one a couple of days before, as I kept in mind. And—according to your Pa's will, the cattle went to you when you came of age. You're the legal owner.

"You see, you ain't rightly a McCale. Our pa died, and Ma married a second time. We ain't never talked about that—we felt mean and jealous. But it was your dad had the property, and we've just been actin' as trustees for you till you came of age."

## Chapter XIII

After the night had swallowed the three, Cal digested what they had told them. He made no attempt to call them back, realizing how uncomfortable they felt in the light of these disclosures. He was beginning, for the first time, to understand how their lives had been twisted and embittered, by what Tom had finally revealed.

As a boy, he'd heard rumors, half-told tales, to the effect that Old Tim McCale had been a good cowboy but a poor cattleman; hard-working, but improvident, with a tendency to gamble away every dollar he made.

No one had ever told him, until now, that his mother had married again, but it was clear that the sons of Old Tim had resented the whole deal, refusing to talk about it or acknowledge him after he, too, had died, cherishing a bitterness which they had more or less unconsciously vented on his son. The fact that the property had been his, and was to be Cal's inheritance when he became twenty-one, had, in their eyes, added insult to injury.

He had no doubt that they had planned to carry out the letter of the will, but that did not lessen their resentment. Now, at the last, in typical McCale fashion, they had, as they would express it, pulled a fast one, by giving a bill of sale which had no legal value. They had followed a twisted set of values for so long that it was hard for them to think straight.

Probably they had overlooked the fact that the joke might be upon Cal, rather than Strang. Everyone counted the Three as the owners; and in the absence of a documented will which declared the contrary, his own coming of age was pointless.

Carrie came to where he stood and placed her arms around him.

"I know this has been a shock to you, Cal," she said. "But we'll get the cattle back," she added fiercely. "The herd belongs to you—and nothing is any worse than it was!"

"That's right," he agreed wearily. "Anything from them was too much to hope for, I guess. I don't particularly blame them—they can't help the way they feel, I suppose. They've not only resented me, but have been jealous because I was the real owner. And that's a joke now, eh? But at least, I won't be taking anything from them. And we'll manage by ourselves."

He was dozing off when a sound brought him awake. Something was there, a shadow where none should have been, wavering between the earth and the high stars. The sensation of fear was as real as though a grizzly or bull buffalo had been outlined, and Cal started to reach for his gun, but checked at a growled warning, coming from behind.

"Hold it, McCale. And reach—high!"

Again the voice had a familiar ring. As he turned his head, he saw that it was Limpy who held the gun. The other, who also kept him covered, was the same man who had ridden with Limpy on the occasion of their last meeting, who had unwillingly led Limpy in a noose.

Apparently they had come through that experience none

the worse, but the memory rankled. Tonight they intended to pay him back.

"I knew our day would come," Limpy informed him. "The trouble with you, McCale, is that you're like your brothers, too pig-headed to quit when the game's played out. Knowin' that, we've been watchin' for you to show up—and sure enough, here you are!"

"Well, now we've got them, what are we going to do?" the other man demanded. "Shoot them, or what? I'd be in favor of hangin' 'em," he added. "Except for such a lack of trees."

"There's ways and ways in which a man can die," Limpy retorted. "Didn't he show us one day, with a rope? I'm keepin' the possibilities in mind."

"All right, but the best method is to get a job done while you have the chance," his companion argued. "I've seen too many good opportunities get spoiled by waiting."

"Nothing's going to go wrong about this one."

Limpy insisted confidently. *"I'm* the one had to endure that rope, and so I don't aim to get this over with too fast. There's such a thing as savorin' what's coming to you. Still and all," he added, "it might be you've got a point. I dunno but what I'd rather dance at the end of a noose, than to be shot—startin', say, with a bullet in one arm. then the other. There's six shells in a gun, which leaves a couple for the legs, and two more for finishin' a man off, but not too fast."

They had made no move to disarm their captives, and McCale knew what Limpy had in mind. Having the drop, he intended to taunt them, hoping they would make a desperation move. That would furnish an excuse to start shooting, and afterward it would proceed somewhat as he had outlined.

Carrie was watching, wordless, her face a white blob in

the gloom. So far, they had no suspicion that she was a woman. Aside from that, the situation could scarcely be worse.

"All right, we'll do it either way you say," the second man agreed impatiently. "But let's get on with it and make sure while we got a chance. I been laughed at plenty, and once is enough."

Limpy's face flushed darkly. Not a day had passed since their ignominious return in a rope without several sly remarks concerning their plight. He had brooded, and the manner of his revenge had become an obsession.

"All right," he growled. "Which one do you want? We can't afford no mix-up in this."

"I guess you're hankerin' to start on McCale, so I'll take the little feller. He's kind of a pretty sort of a kid, and I'm curious to see how long he stays so!" The hammer of his gun eared back ominously.

It was probably hopeless, McCale realized; resistance would probably be too slow, if only by a fraction. And once he had a bullet through his gun arm, they could carry out the rest of their program just about as they pleased.

Any appeal for mercy, even for swift death, would be wasted breath with this pair. As if to emphasize that, the second man made his brag.

"I used to ride with Strang when he was a guerilla," he added. "He's tamed down to a shadow of them days, but I ain't forgotten! Believe me, once we lessoned a town, they never needed a second!"

All three of them heard Carrie's indrawn breath. "You wouldn't shoot *me*, would you?" she said, and her next action caught the outlaws by surprise. Like McCale's her arms had been raised. In a sudden gesture, she jerked off her hat and, with a shake of her head, released her hair in a thick, wavy mane. It had not been cut too short to begin with, and in the intervening time it had smoothed out, all raggedness gone. Even without her added words, the revelation was breath-taking.

"You wouldn't shoot a woman, would you?"

Both outlaws gaped, too astonished by the transformation to make a quick readjustment. Cal was also surprised, but he lost no time. Carrie had given him a break, and he threw himself to the side, hand dipping for his revolver.

A volley of shots erupted like thunder from a clear sky. Though startled, Limpy was too old a hand to be taken really off-guard. He had fixed it firmly in his mind that Cal McCale was not only a man to be hated, but that he was dangerous, and must be watched. His attention strayed an instant, then jerked back like the lash of a bull-whip. The crack of his gun matched McCale's.

Thunder ended in almost the time of its beginning, and silence came down as shatteringly. Carrie and himself still on their feet, but the others were down. Carrie's knuckles showed white where they clasped the butt of the revolver, matching her face. The gloom concealed most of the smoke which twisted from its muzzle, but Cal had seen the earlier lance of flame. She had outmatched the guerilla, and his shot had been too fast and wild.

A second time, Cal heard her catch of breath. She moved a slow step, then another, pausing to stare down at her victim. Her voice sounded harsh and strained.

"He—it was him who shot Ma—just as she came to the door. I saw him do it!"

"In that case, you evened the score," Cal returned. "You sure used your head, Carrie."

His voice was even, almost monotonously level, but at something in his tone she turned swiftly, then she was beside him, her face whitening afresh.

"Cal! You're hit!"

He nodded, watching where his gun had slipped from his fingers to strike the ground. A few drops of blood followed, running down his hand, spattering from his fingertips.

"It's not too bad," he protested. "No bones broken, I guess. But he did drill my arm."

To that degree, Limpy's last shot had been a triumph for his fixed resolve. His plan had been to disarm McCale with a shot through the arm so that from then on he could unhurriedly pick his targets. Even in the stress of haste, he had made good to that extent.

The bullet had drilled cleanly through the flesh, above the elbow. The wound and its destructive power could have been far worse; even so, the shock of the heavy bullet was taking effect.

Carrie's teeth showed white against her lower lip, but she gave no other sign of dismay as she unbuttoned his shirt sleeve and rolled it back. Blood was spilling freely from both sides of the arm.

"Yes, I suppose it could be worse," she agreed. "But we've got to check that bleeding. Sit down, while I get something."

As he sank to the ground, he heard the rip of cloth, then she was on her knees beside him, her breath warm against his face, the uncovered strands of her hair tickling his neck. The sharp throbbing of the wound left him dizzy, and there was not much improvement after she bandaged it, except that the bleeding was checked.

"Oh, Cal, I wish I knew what to do," she whispered. "I suppose it should have some salve, or something. Only I—I don't know what, and we don't have a thing."

"It's fine now," he said reassuringly. "It has bled enough to make a clean wound, and that's as good as we could ask. I suppose it will be sore for a while, but that won't matter."

To demonstrate, he got to his feet again, forced to fight dizziness; but it could turn out as he had said, along with a bit of luck. The trouble was that one never knew what might happen with such a wound. Sometimes they healed nicely. Again, all sorts of complications could ensue, and many a man was in his grave for what had seemed no worse than a scratch.

"We'd best move out of here," he added. "Maybe the pair of them were on the prowl, with nothing else to do. On the other hand, their camp may be within the sound of the guns."

Carrie responded with prompt efficiency. A man could ask no better partner on the trail, Cal thought proudly as he moved in turn, somewhat unsteadily. It was a chore to mount, awkward with an injured arm. The horses which the pair had ridden showed against the light, some distance away. They left them to stand.

"We've no need for extra horses, and if anybody saw and chanced to recognize them, they'd be a liability," Cal explained. "This way, when anybody finds this place, all they can do is make a guess at what happened. Likely they'll hit on the truth, that those fellows came on a camp and tried to rob. As to who was in the camp—well, it could have been most anybody."

He doubted if his glib explanation deceived Carrie. Their own hazard would increase, for suspicion would center on them, among the remainder of the outlaw crew. The one good aspect was that there was no sign of the herd or the camp.

"But the cattle can't be far off," he added worriedly. "They must have moved mighty fast on the final leg of the journey."

After a couple of miles, Carrie called a halt. Cal rode, clasping the saddle horn with his left hand. Despite that, he was swaying, the full effects of shock taking effect.

Brush denoted the presence of a spring, and Carrie knew that he'd need cold water. She steadied him down from his horse, then eased him to the grass. She brought water, and he drank thirstily. Tonight, for the first time along the trail, she spread her own blanket near his, and he was dimly aware of her bending above him two or three times in the night. His arm throbbed painfully, and between snatches of sleep, he thought angrily that it was all ridiculous. Such a wound shouldn't trouble him.

By morning, the arm was swollen and painful. Carrie built a fire, heated water, and washed it carefully, before replacing the bandage. Cal realized that he had a touch of fever, and fought against light-headedness. Now, more than ever, he needed to be alert, cool in judgment. Aside from an occasional glimpse of the railroad grade, the country looked as empty as ever, but appearances were deceptive.

It was no longer possible to look far, to an endless horizon. The country now was rolling and broken, a land green and inviting with promise; but a land where enemies could hide with less effort.

He had a disturbing thought as they rode. They were inferring that the herd was somewhere to the west, near the construction town which marked End of Steel. Strang had planned to ship, and that seemed a logical goal. But it might be that he'd heard the bad news concerning the market, so he could easily have changed his plans. The herd might be moving east instead of west, or to some new goal. If that should turn out to be the case, they might never catch sight of the herd again.

He did not mention his fears, for they had to keep going. It would be worse to turn back; the thing to do was to find the town and make certain. They had inferred from the homesteader's tale that it wasn't far, but he could have been mistaken, and distance was often a matter of guesswork.

The day was like a nightmare. Part of the time, Cal

knew that he was light-headed, his thoughts wandering. His arm continued painful, and a time or so he lost his way among the breaks. It was luck to glimpse the sun on the rails, a long way off, but he wasn't thinking straight.

In a rational moment he warned Carrie that they would have to get back to the track and follow it. It was then that he saw the fear in her eyes.

"Oh, Cal, I'm just no help to you at all," she wailed. "I don't know how to go straight, in such country. And you—you're not fit to keep traveling!"

But the corollary to that was that keeping on might be their salvation. Time was running out; and in a town there might be a doctor.

They found the railroad again, and Carrie took charge, camping again in a secluded spot. Cal struggled between reality and fantasy. There were clouds forming in the southwest, weird clouds, but he was not sure how much of that he imagined. Carrie did not trouble him with questions, but she watched with uneasy eyes, until the darkness hid the increasing blackness of the cloud.

An eerie sound brought him awake, clear in mind but with an oppressive sense of wrongness. This time there were no shadowy figures, but there was something else—marching storm, terror which rode the night.

## Chapter XIV

Clouds spilled across the sky, moving like a ragged flock of geese, the arrow dipping and wavering as it advanced, stars glittering at either side. The wind was tearing at the clouds, harrying savagely. Even the half-dark could not conceal the terror wrapped in such a package. Carrie crouched close to Cal, as though both seeking reassurance and fiercely anxious to protect him.

"What can we do?" she asked. Then: "I'm glad you're awake!"

The rain hit as she spoke, blotting out such vision as had existed, smothering lesser sounds in a burst of fury. Water spilled as though the tear in the cloud had upended a lake in the sky. Carrie pressed close, and they clung together, deriving solace from each others' nearness. There was nothing else which they could do, no time or chance to flee, no place to run.

It was difficult to breathe, almost like being in a pond, with heads below the surface. Thunder tore the clouds apart, allowing an eerie light to spill through. The rain slackened, but it was as though it fled before a still more awesome presence—a giant who came with great leaps, one arm reaching for the earth.

The funnel cloud of the tornado seemed to be coming

straight at them, the drag of the wind almost unbelievable. In such a tempest they would be like playthings, to be tossed and discarded. It howled toward them, then, like a jumping jack, feet ahead in the sky, it veered off south and was gone. They were still there, the rain subsiding to a steady beat. Carrie's face seemed to hold the reflected shine of the storm.

"I was praying," she whispered. "Hard!"

"Then I'm sure that helped," Cal agreed. "It would have had us in another ten seconds. But it's the nature of twisters to skip and hop. We're lucky that one veered as it did."

The rain was like a compress against his fever. It might have been the fresh ozone in the air, but he was clear-headed again, for the first time in hours. Had it not been for the increasing soreness of his arm, he would have felt like a new man. But it was impossible to wish away the track of the bullet.

The rain dribbled away, leaving the air raw with chill. They went on, walking, leading the ponies, needing exercise to keep warm, gradually drying in the dawn wind.

At daylight they glimpsed a town, tossed like a mirage at the edge of the prairie. This, beyond any doubt, was the camp at End of Steel, a sprawling conglomeration of tents, shacks, and railroad cars. The raw line of the grade was like a festering scar. At the near-side, stockyards and loading pens had been built, the planks showing fresh and unweathered. The pens stood empty, though vast brown blobs dotted the plain—south, west and north—trail herds which had gotten this far, reaching a mecca only to find it a sinkhole of despair.

The storm had been a near-calamity for the half-finished ant heap of humanity. Streets showed as lanes of mud, along which men were beginning to stir, striving to assess damage, to bring order where the storm had trod.

Tents had collapsed. Even frame buildings showed twisted, one or two unroofed.

As they topped a final slope and obtained a better view, the scene held a grim sort of familiarity. The cattle were everywhere—not just a few herds, but scattered as far as the eye could range, tens of thousands, huddled in clumps, or wandering disconsolately, while no one seemed to care.

"It looks as though the tornado missed the town, the same as it did us," Cal observed. "Apparently it didn't bother the herds off to the west, either, but it must have stampeded some of the other bunches. Now they'll have a job, sorting them out and rounding them up."

Small groups of riders were beginning to fan out, commencing the task. A lot of time and hard work would be involved, with the results appearing nearly pointless, the market situation being as it was.

"It couldn't be better for us," he added. "I'll find a barber and get fixed up to look halfway respectable, then find Strang and have a talk. He should be in a mood to make a deal."

Carrie eyed him dubiously. "Do you think so, with your arm injured the way it is? Anyhow, the first thing you should do is to see a doctor. Your arm comes first."

"All right, we'll try and get all three tended to," he agreed good-naturedly. "I'll put it up to Strang on a fair basis. He's got some claims, and so have I. But right now, he's got a herd that's only a headache to him, and not much chance of selling them anywhere. I've some money, once we get to my place, and if he'll deliver the herd in good shape, I'll make it worth his while. It will make a good deal, all around."

Carrie drew a breath of relief. She had been driven by thoughts of revenge, just as Cal had. But there had been misunderstanding and overmuch of trouble on both sides, and she was suddenly, intensely proud of this man. It required bigness of more than a physical sort to be willing to overlook injuries and do the fair thing. And it just might be that, given the chance, Strang would meet him halfway.

At any rate, it was worth trying, far better than pursuing a quarrel to a bloody climax which must inevitably spell disaster for both sides. The land was big, and for the present there was a surplus of cattle. And here was a man who measured up to the greatness of the opportunity.

"I think it's a wonderful idea, Cal," she said. "I'm proud of you."

"If you like it, that's all that really matters," he assured her.

The town, once they were in it, was even sorrier than it had looked from a distance. Even its boisterous spirit was subdued beneath the sea of mud. Strings of freight cars sat on side-tracks, but there was no activity along the line. No locomotives puffed; nothing stirred. A bystander, picking thoughtfully at his teeth with a golden toothpick, informed them that a fresh trainload of supplies had been expected that morning, but had failed to arrive.

"What it adds up to is that everybody's short of just about everything that a civilized man needs," he said laconically. "The railroad lacks steel, ties, and spikes for laying track. The saloons have run out of liquor. The stores are down to beans with no flour. Beef and beans will keep one from starving, but as a steady diet, it tends to grow monotonous." He hooked the toothpick to a link at the middle of an expansive watch chain. "You say you want a haircut? Well, I'm a barber. Lately, customers have been lacking, but I guess I haven't forgotten how."

He led the way to his shop, and while he prepared to give Cal a trim, Carrie crossed the street to the general store, eager to make some much-needed purchases.

"Even three months ago, everything was booming," the barber said with a sigh. "Never a day passed without at least one man being shot, and most days a mile of track was laid. Now everything's slowed, people have lost enthusiasm. There hasn't been a shooting in three days. Nobody wants a haircut, even. When a bunch of cowboys could head east with a cattle train, they'd want to be all slicked up for the trip. Now, nobody goes east, or anywhere else, what difference does it make?"

Carrie returned, announcing that she had found a doctor, who was awaiting Cal in his office. He went along without protest, for his arm was throbbing again, and the effect of the coolness from rain and storm had worn off. The doctor clucked disparagingly.

"It's a good thing that you got here now, and not an extra day later," he observed. "I'll clean this up, and with luck, we'll have you on the mend again in a few days. But you'll spend the next several days in bed."

Cal shook his head. "I've no time for that," he protested. "Besides, where would I get a bed in this town, the way things are?"

"That's a reasonable question, and as it happens, I can answer it," the doctor assured him. "We have what passes for a hotel, and the proprietor owes me a debt. I'll see that he gives you a room. Regarding the lack of time, that's a besetting delusion with mankind. We all feel that what we have to do is so important that it can't wait—and most times, we're so wrong that it's pitiful.

"If you're a cattle buyer," he went on, taking note of the fresh haircut, "why, you can take all the time you want, and take your pick from a score of herds. But if you had in mind to buy and ship—and you may know that business better than I would even pretend to—still, you won't be shipping out for quite a while. Haven't you heard what happened last night?"

"I guess maybe the news has escaped me," Cal confessed. "Is it any worse than the rest?"

"Well, at best, it's not considered as being an improvement. Everybody has been counting strongly on that supply train arriving today. It has been promised and overdue for days, and now it won't come. You know of that sidetrack, about a dozen miles to the east? It seems that the train was on it, waiting. Only the tornado didn't wait," he added dryly. "That train, and the tracks for a mile around, were ripped up and scattered over the landscape. Which means at least another week before any train can reach town again."

He scowled ferociously at the fresh bandage and shook his head. "That's the best I can do, for the moment. Come along, and we'll see about that room."

He was as good as his word, overriding the landlord's protests, so that Cal was presently ensconced in a reasonably comfortable bed. The doctor added a final word.

"I prescribe rest and good food—but since you will probably resist the one and aren't likely to get the other, don't complain if my handiwork proves as ineffectual as most things around this outpost of iniquity. I signed on, in a misguided moment, to travel along with the railroad, being sure that men would need medical attention, and naive enough to believe that it might be an adventure! Look after him, Lady! We men don't know enough to take care of ourselves."

"I'll do my best," Carrie promised, and watched Cal drop off to sleep. She returned to the street, warm now and beginning to steam under the sun, with more and more activity getting under way. She had been thrilled by the store, which, despite its inadequacies, seemed to her a veritable wonderland, stocked with goods such as she had dreamed of. She had cut short her shopping to seek out the doctor.

Now she returned to the store. Inside, she caught her breath and hesitated, shrinking back as she saw the pair who, standing remotely, were discussing some matter earnestly. One of the two was Strang.

She had seen him only once before, and from a distance, on the morning when her parents had died. As nearly as she could tell, he had been remonstrating, not liking what had happened so swiftly, yet clearly the man in charge. She knew that she would never forget him.

The second man, who in dress and manner had all the earmarks of an Easterner, was speaking impatiently.

"You can count yourself as mighty lucky that I'm even willing to talk business with you, Strang. There are at least half a hundred men around here, each with a trail herd, cattle which are running short of grass, and no place to go with them, no market anywhere. They can't ship east even if they wanted to—and even if they did, what the stock would bring on today's markt wouldn't even pay shipping charges. You know that as well as I do!"

"The market's bound to improve, Olson—likely before the summer's over."

"Sure—in a matter of months, maybe. And what happens in the meantime? But suit yourself. Any of these others would jump at a chance for a cash sale, and I'm not choosy. Only I talked to you first, so I'm giving you the break. Do you want to sell, or don't you?"

Strang shook his head. "Seems as if I haven't much choice," he admitted resignedly. "Come along and look the herd over, and if your offer is even half reasonable —and you have the cash . . ."

Olson nodded briskly. "Fine. I have the cash. I'll be at your camp at noon. As to looking them over, every longhorn out of Texas looks the same, so this shouldn't take long."

## Chapter XV

Brushing past where she stood with only a glance in Carrie's direction, the pair left the store. She looked after them, dismayed. Disaster threatened just when it had seemed as though something might be worked out. Should the herd be sold to a third party, it would be impossible ever to get it back. In this country there was no law, no legal recourse for straightening out such tangles. The cattle would be moved out of the country, hopelessly lost.

Cal would know what to do; there might still be time. The buyer had promised to be at the encampment at noon. She hurried, no longer mindful of the half-dry, clinging mud, scarcely noticing others, until she brought up with a jolt and a gasp as, rounding a corner, she collided with another hurrying pedestrain.

"Oh, I—I'm sorry," she exclaimed. "I didn't mean—I hope you're not hurt . . ."

"Oh, not at all—in fact, I could scarcely think of a more pleasant encounter than with so lovely a young lady on so fair a morning . . ."

He broke off in mid-sentence, looking at her more sharply; then they exclaimed in mutual recognition. It was the doctor.

"So it's you," he observed. "May I inquire the reason for this great haste?"

Carrie flushed. "I was going to see Cal," she explained. "Something has just come up . . ." She stared in dismay. "I almost forgot. I shouldn't bother him now, should I?"

"That would depend on the nature of the difficulty," he replied. "If it is something which might excite him, as much as it appears to have agitated you, or to send him off at such a headlong pace—then I would advise against it. I'll be honest with you," he went on gravely. "What he needs right now is rest and sleep. A couple of days may make all the difference. In one sense, it's not the injury to his arm so much as the effect of the injury."

"I'm afraid I don't quite understand," Carrie admitted.

"Neither do I." The doctor's smile was a trifle wry. "In fact, there are a great many things in connection with my profession which I don't understand. But I have observed how nature works if left to her own devices, and with now and then a mild assist from fellows like myself. Or how nature can react, sometimes violently, if the proper assistance is refused at the right moment.

"What I'm trying to tell you is this. That injury could easily develop into blood poisoning, instead of healing. I've seen similar cases go both ways. Too much excitement and exertion, and the blood appears to develop a ferment which it cannot throw off. On the other hand, a couple of days of rest, allowing nature to work its own healing, may see him as good as new—instead of in his grave." He bowed, smiling again. "If I can be of any help, whatever your problem may be, instead of exciting him at this point . . ."

"No, thank you," Carrie refused. "I'll find a way to manage—and thank you very much." She went on more slowly, then turned about and headed back to the store.

Why not? She had planned something along similar lines by herself, and probably much more dangerous. Since this was for Cal, she must not hesitate.

Cal had planned to try to settle matters amicably, to make some sort of a deal. In discussions along the trail, he had revealed some of his original plans when he'd first headed toward Texas—to buy cattle, and how much he could afford to pay. She would use her best judgment, and she could do no less than try.

She made her purchases, then returned to the barber shop, to the manifest surprise of the barber. Somewhat dubiously, he conceded that he could give her the sort of haircut she desired, but he was plainly disapproving as he snipped off her locks. Her explanation that long hair on the trail was only a nuisance left him unconvinced.

"Likely you're right, ma'am," he admitted. "Still, it's a sin and shame to cut hair as pretty as yours. But if that's what you want—why, it's your hair."

Looking at herself in the mirror, to note the effect, she was both shocked and elated. She had a conviction that Cal would not like it, but the hair would soon grow out again. Properly attired, she should make a quite passable-appearing man—or at least a boy.

"Though a boy won't do," she reminded herself. "I've got to look and talk and act like a man—and convince them! And this way, they'll never guess who I am."

To her infinite relief, Cal was still sleeping when she returned to the room. It would be hard to explain to him without exciting him, especially if he understood what she had in mind. But the cumulative effects of illness and exhaustion seemed to have caught up with him. Rest now, as the doctor had said, could mean the difference between life and death.

She changed to the new clothes, boots and jeans, shirt and hat, then hurried out again. Time was short. Their horses were at a livery barn a couple of blocks from the hotel. Sun and wind were drying the mud, but the sun was also approaching its zenith.

Inquiry revealed that the big herd with the Muleshoe brand was not too far away. A cattleman, obviously a Texan, pointed it out politely. She got her own horse, the startled stableboy looking twice at this transformed figure. He shook his head, but, remembering her face, raised no protest.

Exactly what she would say or do, Carrie was not at all certain. She would go as Cash Dulane, and she would be in competition with the man who called himself Olson —quite obviously because that was not his name. Beyond that, everything was new and uncharted.

She could not very well explain to Strang that she was representing a McCale, for that would certainly increase the complications. Olson would probably be a formidable antagonist at bargaining, more to be feared than Strang or the trail wolves who followed at his heels. Here at the edges of civilization, they would be at pains to show good behavior. Strang was anxious to sell, to be rid of a herd which had turned out to be both an increasing problem and disappointment.

Thinking about Olson, she was increasingly worried. He professed to be a cattle buyer, probably representing some eastern syndicate, and perhaps he was. He looked and dressed the part, but somehow, in her eyes, he did not fit the pattern.

*Likely I'm foolish to even think that I know much about such things,* she thought. *But he doesn't look or sound like a Skowegian! . . . I've got it! He sounds just like white trash in the Ozark hills! And I'll bet that's what he is.*

But instinctive mislike and distrust would be of no help. Plainly, Olson wanted to get hold of this particular trail herd. But why? As he had been at pains to point out, plenty of other herds were equally available.

*If I knew why, I could beat him,* she thought. *But I don't know, so I've got to win anyhow.*

All that she could do was to make an offer. Against that, Olson had boasted that he had cash in hand, and if he produced the money, what could she do to counter it? Strang's decision, given such a choice, was almost foregone.

The herd, as she approached, was grazing peacefully. None of the bunches hereabouts had been stampeded or scattered by the big wind. The cook was busy at his perennial occupation, and savory odors were beginning to drift on the breeze.

On the trail, hot meals came at morning and night, though rarely at noon. But with time on their hands, no liquor obtainable in town, and the let-down from work, men soon grew bored. The rest and a sleep to which they had looked eagerly forward was already beginning to pall. At such a time, one method for keeping men contented and out of trouble was to keep them well fed, even if the fare was only beefsteak and beans.

The cook was working between two wagons, and at sight of the one, Carrie's breath caught. She had journeyed in that from Missouri to Texas, thence on to the Nations. Following that bloody dawn at the homestead, the trail crew had appropriated it. She blinked back tears, then set her jaw.

Men were sprawled about, waiting for the chuck call. Dismayed, she recognized Olson, well ahead of time. Had he already completed a deal?

The others watched curiously as she rode up. Striving to act assured, she jumped down from her horse, then strode across to the group. She had smudged a corner of cheek and jaw with dirt, hoping it might help hide the absence of whiskers.

Everyone was turning to look. She halted, hands on hips, surveying them half-challengingly. "I'm looking for a man named Strang," she announced, and was pleased that her voice came out deep and somewhat gruff. "I'm Cash Dulane."

Strang came to his feet. He stood a moment, undecided, almost inclined to tip his hat, but forbearing.

"I'm Strang," he admitted. "What can I do for you, Dulane?"

"I'm here to buy cattle—a good-sized herd. I heard in town that you had one to sell. I represent an outfit in Montana. We have plenty of graze, but need stock."

Strang's face showed quick interest. Apparently the deal with Olson was not completed, and just as clearly, it had not been going to Strang's liking. To have competition was a windfall.

"You're correct to the extent that the herd is for sale—if the price is right," he nodded.

Olson came suddenly to his own feet. Until now, he had watched with an air half-wary, half-amused. Quickly he voiced a protest. "Now see here, Mr. Dulane," he exclaimed. "I've already made a deal for this herd . . ."

He caught Strang's sardonic glance, and checked.

"A deal, Olson?" Strang repeated. "Certainly we've discussed one—but we haven't made any. I told you your offer was mighty low, even for times like these. If this gentleman cares to better it, I'm listening."

"That depends, of course," Carrie was beginning to feel more assured. At least, they did not suspect that she was a girl, and while they might think her youthful for such a job, Olson's quick protest had helped give her stature.

"You have about two thousand head, I believe?"

"Roughly that."

"And you can furnish title, of course?"

"I have a bill of sale, signed by the former owners."

"Good enough, I guess. There's another thing. If we make a deal, I'd prefer to have your crew deliver them to the ranch in Montana, on the Yellowstone. Cash on delivery."

"Since Mr. Olson also wants us to deliver them, that's good enough—if we make a deal," Strang admitted. "What's your offer?"

Carrie started to draw a deep breath, then checked it in the middle. She mustn't appear too eager.

"Ordinarily, cattle are worth about eight dollars a head, averaging through a herd," she pointed out. Cal had expounded on the subject one day at some length. "But right now, if you ship east, you won't get enough to pay the costs. But cattlemen should give each other as fair a deal as possible. You've already driven all the way up from Texas. By next year, we hope that the market will recover, and it should. So we'll split the difference between what they were worth, and nothing—which is the other alternative. Say four dollars a head, for the number delivered."

Strang was a gambler, and his face told nothing. He merely looked at Olson expectantly.

The latter did not hesitate. He seemed to have regained his confidence, listening almost with amusement. "All right, Strang, so I offered you three dollars," he admitted. "With plenty of cattle for sale at almost any price, a man has to protect himself. But I'll match this, er—young man, and his offer. Four dollars, delivered."

Strang looked back to Carrie, and now the excitement was beginning to show in his eyes. "We seem to have dead heat," he suggested.

"Five dollars," Carrie said quietly. "That's the best I can do."

Olson shrugged. "I'll match it," he said. "I've never let a beardless boy outbid me yet. But five is my top, too."

Carrie waited. She sensed that Strang preferred her offer, but he was anxious for the best deal to be had. At best, the whole venture, from winning the Muleshoe in a poker game to stealing the herd, had turned out disappointingly.

"Then it looks like I get the herd," Olson observed blandly. "I did suggest payment on delivery—and I'll still require delivery before half of the price is paid. But I also told you that I had the cash—and money talks. Or perhaps my young friend would also like to put up—or shut up?"

He drew a hand from a pocket of his coat, and a sort of sigh went up from the onlookers, Strang included. For he clutched what was hardest to come by these days, and most eagerly sought—a handful of bills, of large denomination.

"Here's five thousand dollars, *cash!*" he said triumphantly. "To bind the bargain!"

## Chapter XVI

Like the others, Carrie stared at the money, fascinated. During and since the war, times had been hard, and money was difficult to come by—something talked about but seldom seen. A man with two coins to jingle in his pocket had the illusion of riches. Deals, or bets, even such large-scale ones as Cal's brothers and Strang had indulged in, were usually on a barter basis, with little or no cash involved.

The coming of the railroad, building west across the mid-continent, had seemed for a while to offer the promise of a new era of prosperity. But now, at least temporarily, that bubble had been pricked, and money remained almost a myth, an illusion.

Except this. What Olson held in his hand was tangible. He rippled the bills with the fingers of his other hand, allowing the denominations to be seen. His smile was smugly mocking.

"I hate to disappoint my young friend," he observed, "but he can perhaps find other cattle for sale, on a basis of hope and promise. I'm sure that you, Mr. Strang, as a practical businessman, prefer solid guarantees—such as this cash!"

Strang glanced at Carrie, then as quickly away.

"Money talks," he acknowledged. "And I must admit that it has been far too long a time since I heard any of it."

"Then, if you'll count this—we'll consider the deal as sealed," Olson suggested, and extended the bills.

Strang reached for the money, then stared as Carrie snatched the bills before he could grasp them. Olson glared angrily.

"I don't like your conduct or methods of doing business, Mr. Dulane," he protested. "And some things are difficult to excuse, even allowing for youth or inexperience. If this is your idea of a joke . . ."

"Joke?" Carrie repeated. "It's hardly a joke when you try to cheat a man with counterfeit money! Maybe you haven't seen much money lately, Mr. Strang, but take a good look at this! I happened to be in the Ozarks last winter, while there was a good deal of counterfeit being passed around, and I saw some of it!"

Olson's air of triumph faded. He looked dismayed and uncertain, as Strang took the money and looked at it closely, his face hardening as he made sure that Carrie was right.

"C-counterfeit?" Olson stammered, and was too dismayed to offer a denial. "B-but it can't be. I've been rooked. Why, if it's counterfeit, I'm ruined!"

"I doubt that," Strang's voice was icy. "This is a good imitation, and I'll admit that I would probably have been fooled but for the sharp eyes of my young friend here. But I doubt if you've been fooled, after carrying the money around with you for some time. Though I suppose we have to give you the benefit of the doubt."

Olson gazed around at the faces of the others, all of whom had come to their feet and crowded close. He saw far less sympathy than in Strang's.

"I—I don't understand how it could have happened." But because he understood their mood, he turned with as much dignity as he could muster. "Since you seem unwilling to take my word, and I have nothing with which to bargain, I'll be going," he managed. "I would never have believed it, that I could be deceived in such fashion —ruined..."

He broke off, then, reaching his horse, scrambled into the saddle and rode away, quickly urging it to a gallop. The others looked at Strang questioningly, but he only shrugged.

"Let him go," he decided. "He might be telling the truth. Anyhow, we can't string him up for such an offense, not without proof. Since we didn't get cheated, thanks to Mr. Dulane, it doesn't matter too much."

Carrie was shaky with reaction. Here was victory, at the moment when it had seemed that her try was to end dismally. She had acted on impulse—what her father would have called a hunch. Certainly, in her experience, she had seen so little money as to be anything but familiar with it or what it looked like, either counterfeit or real. The handful of bills which Olson had displayed so confidently might have been either.

It had been partly the manner in which he flaunted them, coupled with the improbability that any man would be carrying so much money around, that had given her the notion. Cash money was a rarity; she supposed there were people who had enough of it, but even those who did—and particularly those who did—were extremely careful as to how they handled or displayed it. For a man to carry so much cash in this country was unusual, to say the least.

What she had said about counterfeit money in the Ozarks was true. There had been a lot of excitement caused by phony bills, supposedly made by someone in that section of the hills. And Olson talked like a native of the Ozarks, not like a Scandinavian.

On sudden impulse, she, too, had gambled. It had been

Olson's sense of guilt which had trapped him, as much as anything else.

She wanted to laugh, to cry, but dared yield to neither impulse. Strang and his partners were suddenly anxious to co-operate, to show their appreciation for what she had done. They agreed to take the herd on as far as the Yellowstone, payment to be made on delivery. Carrie promised to join them somewhere along the way, before their destination was reached.

Turning back, she was both elated and depressed. She had acted a masquerade, not at all as she had originally intended, but she had pulled it off and saved the herd. Cal should be pleased.

But would he? Had she promised too much, virtually in his name? In any case, she must be getting back to him. If he should wake up and find her gone . . .

The sky, bright with sun a short time before, was suddenly overcast, darkening ominously. A second tornadic storm was unlikely so hard on the heels of the other, but heavy rain was definitely a possibility. It was beginning to fall as she reached the edge of town.

The stableboy, taking her horse, offered a word of advice.

"Better duck inside and wait a spell. Looks like it's really going to pour. You'll get soaked 'fore you can get anywhere."

"I don't have far to go, and I'll have to risk it," Carrie returned breathlessly. "Anyway, I'm quite wet already." She set out, almost running. The sky was nearly as black as it had been when the earlier storm had come roaring across the land, and she saw that others had heeded the warning and taken cover. Except for herself, the streets were suddenly deserted. It was still short of midafternoon, but already half-dark, an eerie gloom split abruptly by the slash of lightning, a thunderclap which seemed to set the earth quivering, releasing rain in sheets.

The stableboy had been right; she was drenched, gasping for breath, fighting her way ahead. But she was not the only one foolish enough to be abroad. Someone else walked, head sunk broodingly, as though oblivious of the storm, a figure who turned to stare sharply as she approached. Then, with a savage exclamation of rage and triumph, he leaped at her.

Carrie had just time to recognize a vengeful Olson, to give a choked scream as his hands closed on her throat. Then the sound was cut off by the throttling grip, and the storm-drenched gloom seemed intent on hiding what was taking place.

Cal sat up in bed, momentarily confused. It required a moment to adjust to such surroundings, for it had been a long while since he'd slept in a regular bed, or even inside four walls. He swung his legs over the side and sat up, reaching for his boots and tugging them on. It was vaguely dark, suggesting that he must have slept the day away. A sense of uneasiness seemed to pervade the air like smoke.

Moving to the window, he understood part of the feeling. It was the darkness of approaching storm which cloaked the land, rather than the easy onfall of night, and at such moments there was always an oppressive sense of threat, as though nature itself waited for what was about to happen. He turned back, wondering in sudden anxiety where Carrie might be. Probably she had gone out, but she might get soaked, and his feeling of unease increased. Then he checked at something in the corner.

There was little furniture in this primitive, barely adequate hotel room—only the bed, a chair, an empty box with a tin bowl and tin pitcher inside the box. Carrie had folded her old garments as neatly as possible and placed them inside the box also, out of sight. But he saw them as he turned.

His first reaction was one of tenderness. The trail had been hard on clothes, and she had badly needed new garments. Apparently she had outfitted herself. Then the sense of uneasiness returned. She had promised, reluctantly, to get what she must have and no more, knowing how little money they had. It looked as though she'd gotten a lot more than she had said.

That was unlike Carrie. She was one to ride the trail with. There, more than anywhere, you came to know a person, how they stacked up. The weak, the whining, and the incompetent showed quickly for what they were. So, too, did character reveal itself. Carrie was unselfish, generous to do her part, dependable.

He had a hunch that something was wrong.

Making sure of his gun, he let himself out of the room. The sleep had done him good, just as the doctor had promised. He found the landlord in the room which served him both as office and living quarters.

The landlord turned from looking out through the open door. Recognizing Cal, he nodded gloomily. "Another storm coming," he observed. "Here we go for more'n a month without a drop of rain, and the whole country startin' to burn up, everybody wishin' it'd rain. Then last night it nigh washes us off the map. And now it has to overdo things some more . . ."

Cal interrupted, his sense of anxiety stronger. "I just woke up," he said. "Have you seen my—my wife?"

It sounded better that way, as well as saving the need for explanations, which were nobody's business. And Carrie would be his wife as soon as they came across an itinerant sky pilot.

The landlord nodded, as though sharing the same anxiety. "Why yes, I did," he conceded. "I was down the street a ways, a couple or three hours back. Saw her ridin' out south. Kind of surprised me. Unless she gets back in a hurry, she'll be in for a wetting."

"Riding south?" Cal repeated, dismayed, and the probable explanation burst on him. It would be like Carrie to seek to save him trouble and risk, expecially since he had been ordered to take things easy. But if she was trying to do business with Strang . . .

He went outside, aware that it was already raining, but heedless of it as he swung toward the livery barn. He'd have to get his own horse; after that, it would be a matter of luck—of hoping that he wasn't too late.

He had covered half the distance when he heard the outcry. Though choked short off, it was Carrie's voice, and he plunged ahead in the thickening curtain of storm.

Olson was appalled. Rage and fear in nearly equal mixtures are not a pleasant emotion, and the one had added to the other as he spurred back to town, apprehensive that the crew might repent of letting him go, vengeful against the brash youth who had not only ruined his scheme but had placed him in such jeopardy. Seeing the cause of his troubles, with the untimely gloom to blanket everything, he had acted on impulse; it had seemed a perfect chance to settle scores. Perfect, until he had realized that it was a woman he held, and not a mere youth.

It was a relief, under such circumstances, to fling her aside and swing at the man bearing down upon him, one hand moving fast, lifting his gun barrel while his finger slid along the trigger.

## Chapter XVII

This was a frontier, bordered and almost literally embroidered by guns. Few, and counted among the foolish, were those who did not possess a weapon; most men lived, or died, by their skill with a gun, or the lack of such ability. Cal McCale had, with no false modesty, rated himself well up the scale.

But today his arm was sore, slow with its injury. With his gun in the holster as Olson lunged out of the gloom, he'd be no match for him in such a contest.

Knowing it, Cal twisted, doubting if his ruse would serve, but taking the only choice. He heard the voice of the gun and sensed its outreach as lead plucked urgently at his sleeve, hemstitching a pattern of holes on the inner side, yet somehow missing. Then he swung his uninjured arm, and with Carrie's cry in his ears, it was like the stroke of a grizzly's paw. Olson went rolling in the mud.

Storm and darkness could be friendly. Olson took advantage of them, rolling to his feet and keeping on without a backward glance, swallowed in the gloom. Cal drew Carrie to her feet and into his arms.

"Carrie!" he cried. "Are you hurt?"

She clung to him, shaking, only the negative movement of her head against his chest answering his question.

Then, remembering the shots at point-blank range, she pulled back and regarded him anxiously.

"I'm fine. But you—were you hit again?"

"Not even a scratch," he reassured her, and believed it, until later he found the burn where a bullet had passed along the inside of his arm. "I didn't have time to stand still."

"Oh, Cal, Cal," she sobbed. "You always come when I need you!"

The landlord greeted them with relief when they returned to the hotel.

"There's a sayin', mad as a wet hen," he observed. "I've noticed that a wet hen usually looks mighty woebegone, 'stead of aggravated—and you two look twice that soaked! But you don't seem to mind."

"Why, no," Cal assured him. "We don't mind at all."

In their room, he listened incredulously while Carrie poured out her story, omitting nothing.

"Did I do right?" she asked anxiously. "I didn't dare wait, for he'd have had the herd—and I suppose that was why he was so mad at me, for spoiling his deal and showing him up! Though when he found out that I was a woman, I could tell how surprised he was. I'm sure he hadn't planned to strike a woman."

"You've done a fine job," Cal assured her. "Probably better than I could have managed. We'll let them get pretty well up the trail before we join them again, just so that it wouldn't pay to change their mind. But don't ever take such risks again!"

Setbacks could be annoying, but in Olson's book they did not greatly matter if permitted to be no worse than temporary detours along the trail. And since, in his own eyes, he was both a genius and a man of parts, he saw no reason to despair.

Despite the day's setbacks, he had once again proved his point. Neither Strang nor his partners had recognized him, though he had gone boldly among them. He counted himself not so much a master at disguise as a perfectionist at playing a new character to the life. The quirk of an eyebrow, the twist of a mustache, the inflection of a voice often worked better than a false beard or a gold cap to a tooth.

And Strang should have remembered him, since it was he from whom Strang had robbed—now a good many years ago—the buckskin bag of precious stones, which Olson, in turn, had taken from another man who, just as falsely, called himself by the same name. But since possession counted as ownership, Olson had never accepted the loss with good grace, or as final.

Time and circumstance had contrived to delay attempts at recovery. There had been the matter of a long stretch in a Missouri jail, a laughable quirk of Lady Luck which he had failed to appreciate—that, too, had been a matter of mistaken identity, and he'd served for another man's crime. (He could have cleared up the confusion as to identity at any time of his choosing; but that would have meant an even longer sentence for a crime definitely of his own commission.)

Afterward, it had taken a long time to discover the whereabouts of Strang, now going under a different name and identity; and to finally convince himself that the jewels might still be around, a prize worth a further try and almost any amount of risk.

Thus it had been no chance which had caused him to select Strang's particular outfit when making an offer for the herd. Possessed of ample funds in bogus bills, the final fruits of a venture which had made the Ozarks too hot a land in which to linger, the beef herd had been incidental, but necessary.

In the bright sun of a new day, he considered the possibilities, then rode hopefully out of town, heading north, as the herd had already done. He planned to meet up with the herd again before many days passed, and he was confident in his new role as Hannibal King.

The day was bright under a not-too-warm sun, the land green and inviting. Olson felt a pang of nostalgia, of which he was not ashamed. He liked to consider himself a man of sentiment, and this, in a way, was homecoming. There were compensations for temporary setbacks.

It had been half a decade since he'd tired of one episode among many, that of life as a squaw man. Always a loner, tribal life had become irksome, so he had left. Now, if opportunity offered, he might renew old acquaintances, especially if they promised profit. If Running Bird was still alive, she'd probably be glad to see him again. Women were that way, squaws especially.

The railroad, with its problems, was well behind when he encountered the wagon train.

No longer did he present the guise of a cattle buyer. He played the part in which he was most at home, that of a man who, across the years, had become more native to his adopted country than a native himself. Even he was temporarily puzzled by two conflicting banners of dust which, drifting miles apart, stained the otherwise clear air.

There was only a little dust; still, it was there for trained eyes to see, and Olson's vision approximated that of a hawk.

There were a dozen wagons in the immigrant train, and it explained the mystery. The other drift of dust was inevitably the herd. Olson rode boldly to join the wagons, confident of a welcome, taking note of how worn and seedy was the outfit. Clearly, they had come a long way in their quest for land, and hard times rode with them.

He had found that to be the rule rather than the exception. The well-planned, well-managed trains were few. Most people were impractical dreamers, many too lazy or improvident to make a success anywhere; such people dreamed of bettering themselves in a new location, and rushed eagerly into rash adventures, lacking not only proper equipment but knowledge. Some made it, but many more met disaster along the way. Olson surmised shrewdly that this was that sort of a train, and not far short of failure.

Their trouble was that they had passed the point of no return; they could neither turn back nor halt. They had to keep on, no matter what might lie ahead.

They watched between suspicion and hope as he rode in, which gave way to welcome as they made sure that he had friendly intentions, and might be able to assist them. He introduced himself as Hannibal King, a footloose man, bound nowhere in particular. Sometimes he acted as guide for wagon trains.

Wistfully, he confessed to a sort of homesickness. They had the right idea—to find land, make a settlement, create homes, to cause the wilderness to flower.

Before the campfire burned out, he had accepted their offer to go on with them as guide, and perhaps, when they settled, to be one with them. They confided that his coming was providential.

While not exactly lost, they lacked a guide who knew the country. Also, of late, they'd had an added worry. Rumors drifted like dawn mist across the land, reports that the red men were restless, often hostile. The newcomer's claim that he knew Indians, and how to deal with them, was reassuring.

Olson quickly demonstrated his competence, noticeably improving the operating procedure. By the second evening, as if by accident, he managed to have the wagons make camp alongside the trail herd.

Arriving in such guise, he had no trouble with Strang or any of the others. They accepted him as Hannibal King. That evening, the hungry settlers feasted on beef steaks, and the crew enjoyed biscuits.

That had been one of the wagon train's problems. They carried an oversupply of flour, but they had been desperately short on many essential items.

The encounter with the trail herd seemed providential, and by the next morning, Olson succeeded in implanting the idea, having it discussed and then eagerly accepted by both sides. Since the cattle and the settlers were both bound north, why not go on together, pooling their resources? At least until they were through the country of the Pawnee.

The next few nights afforded Olson the opportunity he sought. In Catclaw, he'd pieced together the story of how the diamonds had been kicked around and supposedly lost; the first part he could accept, but not the second. Whatever else they might be, the Three Tough T's had shown themselves shrewd gamblers. So the jewels must be somewhere with the herd, and sooner or later, Tom, Tim, and True would plan to retrieve what they had cached.

Which was well enough; only, he intended to be ahead of them.

After the others were asleep, he prowled the wagons —the chuck wagon of the Muleshoe, and, as a precaution, the second wagon which the rustlers used. He wasted little time with a search of the obvious. All such places would long since have received a thorough going-over. Instead, he tapped the heavy bolsters, or, using a brace and very long, small bit, bored holes deep into the wood. The betraying marks he later daubed with dirt, making sure that no trace of shavings remained to disclose the operation.

The trouble was that he found nothing. The borings struck only solid wood, disclosing no secret, hollowed-out compartment where a buckskin sack of unusual weight might be cached.

He worked patiently, thoroughly, overlooking no possible place big enough for such a cache. With increasing frustration, he was forced to conclude that his calculations had been wrong. Either the McCales had told the truth about losing the loot or else they had already retrieved the jewels. Though reluctant to accept either conclusion, apparently it had to be one or the other.

Disgruntled, he turned his thoughts to salvaging something from the wreckage of his hopes.

A small, disgruntled band of Pawnees were raiding, attacking where opportunity offered, acquiring scalps and confidence. With success, more braves were stealing away to join them.

Hannibal King, sometimes known as Olson, at other times as Horse Which Kicks, was a blood brother to the Pawnee, a member of the tribe. Once that had been an aggravation and a hindrance, but now it might be turned to account. For a man wise in Indian lore, the signs were there to read. This time, it was not even necessary to lose sleep, or to make another nocturnal ride. As guide, Olson merely rode off on a scout, met a man, and exchanged a few words. That was enough for the preliminary, and he returned to camp well satisfied.

There he found uneasiness. Cowboys and settlers were deep in discussion. There were other eyes nearly as sharp as Olson's, and some had glimpsed furtive figures who skulked and watched from the horizon—and if these watchers were Pawnees, it might indicate the likelihood of an attack.

He spoke reassuringly. It was true that there were Indians in the vicinity, and that was not surprising, for this was Indian country. Because of the threat, he had scouted carefully. For the present, at least, there was no danger. Should there be, he'd make sure that they were ready in time.

He convinced them, but he knew that it was time to move fast. Already, some of them seemed to be having second thoughts about himself as an addition to the party, or as a guide. Well, let them think what they liked. By the time they woke up to reality, it would be upon them.

He stole away from camp under the cloak of darkness. Sure of himself, he failed to notice when a second shadow detached itself from the huddle of wagons and followed.

He met Old Monte at a point of rocks a mile from the camp. Old Monte had been a dissolute character most of his days, a squaw man for the last dozen years. If not friends, they had been casual acquaintances during Olson's days as a tribal member.

Like himself, Monte could speak Pawnee, but he still found English more to his liking. So in that tongue they made the arrangements.

"The Chief is agreeable," Monte confirmed. "He is willing to let the cattle pass. All that we require are the scalps of the settlers—and the loot from the wagons."

"With the grass springing green, the cattle are in good condition, and your people may feast upon them also," Olson countered. "To the number required for a good meal. Afterward, I will need young men to drive the herd."

"That will be done."

"And the hour of the attack?"

"Tomorrow night, short of the dawn."

"Good hunting," Olson returned, and turned back toward the camp. He had covered half the distance when he glimpsed what might have been a lobo or other animal, but watching closer, he saw that it was a figure who hurried stealthily to return ahead of him.

Olson stared in disbelief. Double-dealing had become so much a part of existence that he took precautions automatically. How anyone could have followed, to eavesdrop, he did ntt understand.

Yet clearly it had been done. The figure that hurried ahead, trying to regain the camp, could have come from nowhere else. And if he succeeded in telling what he knew . . .

What he had to do was risky, but the only way. This time, Olson's gun did not miss. He was standing above the fallen man, smoking gun in hand, when others came rushing up, wakened by the shots and terrified that the Pawnees were upon them. Olson spoke between anger and regret.

"I saw him stealing off, and that made me suspicious, so I trailed him. He was heading to meet an Indian—and when I called for him to stop, he started to run instead. I sure hated to shoot, but we can't have a traitor among us. It just wouldn't do."

## Chapter XVIII

McCale rode warily, every sense on the stretch, taking advantage of every break or patch of brush, making sure that the horses merged with the blacker shadows. This was Pawnee country, and every sign indicated that riders were on the prowl. If a further warning had been needed, it was given by their own horses. The wiry little ponies, descendants of a long line of half-wild cayuses, were possessed of a strong instinct for self-preservation. Sensing danger, they repressed even snorts of distrust; like a moose, which can tip back its antlers and scoot silently through thick woods, they seemed able even to muffle the beat of their hoofs.

"We must be getting close to the herd, so we ought to catch up soon," Cal whispered reassuringly to Carrie who rode beside him. Her hand stole out to grip his in the gloom, clinging tightly an instant. "And it can't be any too soon," he added under his breath.

His troublesome arm had delayed them several days past what they had expected, there at the end of steel. The doctor had shaken his head over its angry red, and Carrie had strongly seconded his insistence that they must not travel until the danger flares subsided. Since they could out-travel the herd several days to one, Cal had conceded.

But now, again several days on the trail, he was anxious to come up with the herd. Quite fresh sign showed where a wagon train had joined and was traveling with the herd, and in that added strength there was a measure of comfort.

"Cal! Someone is there—do you see . . ."

Carrie bit her tongue, realizing that she had broken the rule by speaking aloud; on a still night, sounds carried far. Even an expert, hostile ear would have difficulty in sorting out most noises, and to classify them accurately. But talk could not be mistaken.

Proof of that was swift in coming. Someone was there in the gloom, a figure materializing out of the shadows, running toward them with a cry, between desperation and relief.

"Oh, you must be white people! Thank God I've found you!"

It was a woman, face and arms scratched and with clothes torn from desperate passage amid brush and brambles. She stood, looking up at them, trembling with emotion. Dismounting, Cal saw with increasing surprise that she was about Carrie's age. Then Carrie was clasping her, soothing her with soft sounds of reassurance.

"We'll take care of you," she promised. "What's wrong? Are you alone?"

"It's Indians—and black treachery," the girl breathed. "Are you alone?" she went on, and her voice almost broke with disappointment. "I mean, are there just the two of you? I was hoping—you see, I got away from camp hoping to find help. The Indians are to attack before daylight . . ."

"Take it easy, now, so we can get this straight," Cal counseled, and gradually they drew the story from her.

A terrifying thing had happened the night before, doubly shocking to her. She belonged to the wagon train which had joined with the trail herd; so, too, had Jethro Rains. And during the long months of their journey from Indiana, romance had blossomed between them.

The difficulty there was that Jethro, back in Indiana, had belonged to a family with whom the Tuckers had scarcely associated. Imogene's parents had liked his looks no better on this far slope of the sunset.

"But we loved each other—so we managed to meet sometimes," the girl sobbed. "Last night, we stole away from camp, to meet at a point of rocks. We had hardly got there, though, when two other people came along. One was our guide, a man named King, and the other looked like an Indian, though he sounded English."

Crouching in the shadows, she and Jethro had listened, appalled, as the details for the betrayal and massacre had been discussed. At the first opportunity, Jethro had slipped away, hoping to reach camp ahead of Hannibal King and reveal the plot.

After the conspirators had gone, Imogene had followed—just in time to witness the brutal fashion in which the guide made certain that Jethro should not betray what he had discovered.

Terrified—certain that she, too, would be killed before she could tell her story—Imogene had set out in a frantic attempt to get help before it was too late.

She had lain concealed during the day, while a search was made for her; once her hopes had risen that she could tell her story, but instead, she had been forced to crouch in apprehension, for one of the pair of searchers was the guide. By then, she realized, he would have understood that she had been at the tryst, so discovery would be fatal.

With darkness she had kept on, almost despairing, until she had glimpsed shadowy riders and heard words in English.

"We've got to get back," she gasped, "and warn them. Though I'm afraid it's hopeless. There won't be enough of us to fight off the Indians."

"Maybe not, girl—but at least here's three more who can shoot—and will!"

Cal was startled in turn, but as quickly relieved. Not only were the words in English, but the voice was familiar. A trio rode into sight, The Three T's. Even in the gloom, their patriarchal aspect was impressive. Tom explained gruffly.

"We heard voices, and found you. That wan't too hard, since we've been trailin' you most of the way up from the railroad. We got to thinkin' and talkin' among ourselves—and we had to admit that we'd sure let you and the little lady down, Cal, and just when you needed help. So we set out to see if we could remedy that."

Coming from Tom McCale, it was a handsome admission. Tonight, three extra guns might spell the difference in a battle for survival.

The night seemed ominously silent as they approached the camp. Cal observed grimly that no precautions had been taken, such as would be reasonable in Indian country; Hannibal King had maintained the delusion that no risk was imminent.

The dark bulk of the herd showed where they were bedded down, at least a mile from the camp. The dozen wagons were loosely grouped, instead of being formed in a circle for protection. No sentries were awake to challenge their approach.

Conversely, no Pawnees had done so. It was well past midnight, and if Imogene had understood correctly, then attack was imminent. Cal's guess was that this hour of the second night had been chosen because the Pawnees must be coming from a considerable distance.

One wagon stood apart from the others, and at a closer

sight of it, Carrie caught her breath. Silence was no longer necessary, so she spoke.

"That's our wagon, Cal—Pa's old wagon!"

Cal nodded. There was no moon, and the stars stood high and thin. But certain aspects were familiar.

"The rest of you wake up the camp and get them ready," he suggested. "We'll have a look, whether anybody's sleeping here."

It was revealing of his brothers' changed attitude that they offered no protest at his assumption of leadership. They nodded and kept on. Cal stuck his head under the canvas top, making sure that no one was inside. At the front, Carrie leaned from the saddle to touch a link with the past, her face wistful. She thumbed back a hasp and lifted the lid of the boot, or box.

"Why, everything is just as it was when we loaded stuff at the Muleshoe!" she exclaimed breathlessly. "It's crammed with everything that Pa thought we might have use for. Sacks of powder and buckshot, caps for the old muzzle-loader—I don't believe anybody's touched it since!"

"Maybe some of that will come in handy tonight," Cal suggested. "But we'd better get on and join the others."

Already, there was stir and commotion, but no panic, as the word was spread. Then a voice arose, loud, imperatively questioning. He saw Carrie's start of astonishment. "That's Olson—the cattle buyer!" she exclaimed. "What on earth is *he* doing here?"

"What's going on? Has everybody gone crazy?" Anger and apprehension gave a ragged edge to Olson's voice. Here, at almost the last possible moment, the company was being alarmed, warned. They still might be able to put up a fight, and he had been at pains to avoid that. Resistance could be misunderstood; no one knew better than he how treacherous was the path of the double-dealer.

Years before, he'd simply ridden away, leaving the tribe, his responsibilities, and his squaw. Many would remember with disapproval. If the massacre went according to plan, he'd be back in favor. But if the Pawnees came upon a hornet's nest, aswarm with vicious stingers, they might believe that he had led them into the trap. Whatever happened then would be bad, for him.

He swung about and saw McCale swinging down from the saddle, and his face washed blank. Then it was suffused with flooding rage. "So that's it!" he gritted, and wasted no words. Gun talk alone was pertinent now.

It was as though only one gun spoke, the double blast blending. But this time, Cal's gun was in his hand instead of the holster, and that made the difference. Others were coming awake, crowding about, exclaiming and questioning as the guide clawed at the grass. Strang was among them.

"What's going on?" he wanted to know, and he had his answer in the sudden, blood-chilling cadence of the war whoop. It burst at them from close at hand, and a solid wave of horsemen erupted from the gloom and swept forward.

Months on the trail had seasoned the immigrants, and the trail crew had heard the war whoop along the banks of the Canadian. There was no panic, but neither was there time nor chance for an adequate defense.

Cal studied the oncoming column. This cavalry of the plains was not organized according to the standards of the white man, but that in no way lessened its effectiveness, or the fact that it was one of the finest fighting forces the world had ever seen. These Pawnees were well-mounted, well-organized, and efficiently led. They swept in massive attack.

In that, at least, they appeared to be taking a leaf from

the white man's book. Normally, Indian warfare favored riding in an ever-tightening circle about and around a trapped group, firing, decimating the defenders, squeezing shut the noose. When the plan worked, it was deadly; but in that method lay a grave weakness, which determined defenders could exploit. It allowed time for fighting back, and by the laws of existence in such country, the plainsmen were marksmen.

This time, perhaps because of the awareness that the camp was awake, yet certainly in a state of confusion, the warrior chief was leading his men in a headlong charge, intending to sweep over and through the camp, to wipe out all resistance in one swift foray.

They were shouting, firing as they came—rifles which spoke and then kept on firing, modern guns to match the best which might be used against them. They did not have to compete on uneven terms, with smooth-bores and muzzle-loaders, such as Cash Dulane had relied upon.

Answering shots were returned, but they were hasty, ill-aimed. An hour, even half that long, in which to ring the wagons, to organize a defense, might have spelled the difference, but there was no period of grace. Cal wondered despairingly if they had caught up just in time to die with the others.

However few the braves who originally had set out on the glory trail, others had flocked to join them as success attended their efforts. It was an overwhelming horde who rode out of the night. Rifles alone could never break that charge.

A thought leaped like fire in his brain, and at that moment, Carrie was beside him, holding out a heavy rifle. Cal snatched it, but instead of aiming for the warriors, he swung the gun muzzle toward the lone wagon which stood in the path of the Pawnees. It was no barrier, merely a hindrance which they were starting to swing around, splitting like a river at a boulder, to flow around and reunite in irresistible surge.

The odds were long, beyond what gamblers like Strang or his brothers would even consider, but so was the alternative. Cal squeezed off bullets in a roaring stream, his target the wagon which had wheeled the trackless wastes from the Ozarks to Texas, through The Nations, on to this final stand in the heart of the Pawnee country. More particularly, he aimed for the boot, for the close-packed cargo loaded long weeks before from surplus at the Muleshoe—powder and buckshot and caps.

A lucky hit would be his only chance, but he saw the roaring flash, flaring blindingly against the night, before its roar shoved at the eardrums. Concussion hit him as he started to suck in a breath of relief, and Carrie was flung against him by the onrush of air. He caught her with one arm and held her, until the shaking earth regained its poise, and the roar of thunder growled to silence.

That strange hush was broken by cries, mingled with screams and groans. Amid these were the retreating drum of hoofs, the uncertain, disbelieving exclamations of men and women who had looked in the face of death and dared not believe that it would draw back.

The devastation had been far worse than he had dared hope. One of his bullets had torn among the caps to detonate the powder, a bomb jam-packed with sacks of buckshot, bolts and scraps of iron, the whole scattered among the closely grouped warriors.

Half of them would never return from riding the spirit trail. As for the survivors, the surprise of so unexpected and fearful a weapon had shattered their resolution. Those who could were retreating, and they would keep going.

Daylight was coming with a rush of its own, the light

revealing the carnage. But the camp itself was virtually untouched. Strang was first to hold out his hand as he understood, but the Three T's were close behind with the same gesture.

"I don't know quite how you worked it, but you sure saved our bacon," Tom said gruffly. "That was one time I was shakin' in my boots!"

"It strikes me that we've all of us made a lot of mistakes, Tom," Strang suggested. "What do you say if we forget the past and make a fresh start somewhere up this way? And as you said, we can be mighty thankful for the chance."

"I'll go along with that," Tom conceded, and Tim and True nodded concurrence.

The scene of devastation was not pleasant to explore, but Cal did so, along with the others, in the bright light of the sun. Then he stooped, blinked in disbelief, and came up with something which glittered as though to rival the sun.

"I'd hoped to be able to set off that powder, and that the blast might give us a chance," he explained. "But I sure didn't expect it to work half as well as it did. Maybe this is the answer."

In his hand he held a perfect, blue-white diamond, slightly stained with crimson. "Looks like this explains what happened to that sack of jewels that caused so much trouble," he added.

He plucked a ruby from the peppered earth, held it with the other.

"That sack of junk must have got mixed with the other stuff, then was stuffed in the boot, along with other things. From the outside, it would feel like heavy pellets—fine for a muzzle-loader. And nobody ever bothered to look a second time at the stuff stuffed in the boot."

"So that's what happened!" Tom breathed. "I never could quite figure how that disappeared—but all we knew was that it had!"

"Then I owe you an apology, for you were telling the truth," Strang added. "I thought you were, though I couldn't figure you as being quite that crazy!"

"Well, better gather up what can be found," Cal suggested. "Money will still be useful for you fellows. There's room for everybody along the Yellowstone."

"Then that's where we'll start over, if you're willing," Tim agreed. "Close enough to be neighborly, but not underfoot."

"And a share of these belong to you," True added, to which Strang nodded concurrence.

"There's just one thing that bothers me now," Tom suggested almost diffidently. "We've sure got to round up a sky pilot somewhere for you and this little lady!"

Carrie colored, then smiled. To Tom's discomfiture but evident pleasure, she set her hands on his shoulders and gave him a kiss.

"Thank you for the thought, Tom," she agreed. "But that's all taken care of. A parson came in on a train to try and convert the camp—and at least his trip wasn't entirely wasted!"